Wycliffe was still trapped in a limbo between past and present. Instant memories recalled in scenes and phrases that surfaced for a moment and were gone. Francine in the chancel of the village church, wearing a blue gown and caught in the spotlight, singing a lullaby – the Virgin in a nativity play. Francine at Mynhager, leafing through an album of old photographs, pondering over them – intent, lost.

Francine, at the top of the stairs, a gun in her hand, standing over a body which lay in a pool of blood: the body of Gerald Bateman MP, her natural father.

W.J. Burley lived near Newquay in Cornwall, and was a schoolmaster until he retired to concentrate on his writing. His many Wycliffe books include, most recently, *Wycliffe and the Guild of Nine.* He died in 2002.

By W.J. Burley

A Taste of Power
Three Toed Pussy
Death in Willow Pattern
Wycliffe and How To Kill a Cat
Wycliffe and the Guilt Edged Alibi
Wycliffe and Death in a Salubrious Place
Wycliffe and Death in Stanley Street
Wycliffe and the Pea Green Boat
Wycliffe and the School Bullies
The Schoolmaster
Wycliffe and the Scapegoat
The Sixth Day
Charles and Elizabeth
Wycliffe in Paul's Court
The House of Care
Wycliffe's Wild Goose Chase
Wycliffe and the Beales
Wycliffe and the Four Jacks
Wycliffe and the Quiet Virgin
Wycliffe and the Winsor Blue
Wycliffe and the Tangled Web
Wycliffe and the Cycle of Death
Wycliffe and the Dead Flautist
Wycliffe and the Last Rites
Wycliffe and the Dunes Mystery
Wycliffe and the House of Fear
Wycliffe and the Redhead
Wycliffe and the Guild of Nine

Wycliffe
AND THE
GUILD OF NINE

W.J. Burley

An Orion paperback

First published in Great Britain in 2000
by Victor Gollancz Ltd
This paperback edition published in 2001
by Orion Books,
an imprint of The Orion Publishing Group Ltd,
Orion House, 5 Upper St Martin's Lane,
London WC2H 9EA

An Hachette UK company

9 10 8

A CIP catalogue record for this book
is available from the British Library.

ISBN-13 978-0-7528-4384-1

Printed and bound in Great Britain by
Clays Ltd, St Ives plc

The Orion Publishing Group's policy is to use papers that
are natural, renewable and recyclable products and
made from wood grown in sustainable forests. The logging
and manufacturing processes are expected to conform to
the environmental regulations of the country of origin.

Some of the characters in this book made their first appearance in *Wycliffe and the Quiet Virgin.* Here the story, which is complete in itself, tells of what happened to them ten years later.

Chapter One

A day in April

Archer's Guild of Nine was a craft colony on the site of a disused mine on the seaward slope of the moor, west of St Ives. The old buildings, adapted for workshops and living accommodation, were scattered on either side of a disciplined watercourse which, in living memory, had been streamed for tin. The site overlooked the village of Mulfra, and beyond that, under a vast canopy of sky, the sea.

On this particular morning that sky was a pale watery blue with dusky, ragged clouds driven before a stiff onshore breeze. The sun shone fitfully, according to whimsical changes in the pattern of those scurrying clouds.

'Nothing doing in wood-carving this morning?'

'Paul is ready to varnish his frieze and he's having a clean-up. You can hardly breathe for dust.' Francine was perched on one of the benches, legs dangling.

Alice Field assembled the exquisite little elements of a miniature four-poster bed, and as she attended to joining and alignment her conversation was sporadic.

In addition to a couple of already assembled four-posters, her bench was littered with little groups of chairs, tables, presses and chests; all to a scale of one-twelfth. No metrication nonsense in this workshop.

'So, how does it feel, living over the job?'

Francine considered. 'All right, I suppose. It saves me the trip in and out every day. Don't you find that a bit of a bind?'

Alice put down her bed, examining it with a critical eye. 'Not really. I like to get away from this place. In any case, Tom wouldn't stand for living on the site even though it would save us money.'

With total objectivity, Francine wondered what it might be like to be 'us'.

Two women talking while one of them worked.

Francine, in her middle twenties, slim, pale of skin, with red-gold hair, had a face which, at that other time, might have launched those thousand ships. Her expression was pensive, withdrawn, giving nothing away.

Alice, perhaps a year or two older, was plump, fair and outgoing. 'Who's buying this lot?' Francine had slipped off her perch and was examining two Lilliputian houses under construction on another bench.

' "This lot", as you call it, is part of an order from the States for five fully furnished houses.' A touch of pride.

Alice picked up the prepared elements of another four-poster and set to work on the assembly. 'Our Lina knows how to drum up business; I'll say that for her. Must be her Dutch blood.'

The window of the workshop looked out on a stretch of moorland, a shallow depression with scattered buildings which had once been part of the mine complex. Close at hand was a large sign at the entrance to the site. There was a logo, depicting Sagittarius firing his arrow, and an inscription:

The Archer Guild of Nine.
Craft Workshops.
Visitors by appointment.

Francine was still examining the little houses. 'I can imagine kids making short work of these.'

'They're not for kids; they're for adults.'

Francine was incredulous. 'You mean grown-up people spend good money on dolls' houses? . . . They must be kinky!'

Alice was piqued. 'It's nostalgia for childhood, Fran. But I doubt if you ever had one.' She paused to make a tiny adjustment to the joining. 'I can imagine your first thought when you entered this world and opened your little eyes. "Is all this on the National Health or are we paying for it?"'

Alice laughed at her own joke. Francine smiled. 'Very funny?'

Alice said, 'Getting back to basics and being nosey, was it Paul's idea that you should move into the flat over the workshop?'

'I don't know what you mean.'

'Oh, come off it, Fran! You can't pretend that the two of you living with his mother and the rest didn't cramp your style.'

'The move wasn't Paul's idea; it had nothing to do with him.'

'How old is Paul?'

'He's twenty-seven, a year older than I am. Why?'

'Isn't it about time the two of you made up your minds? It's no business of mine but playing the field doesn't endear you to the women. I suppose you know there's talk about you and Emile?'

'Emile! Francine was roused. 'But that's nonsense! He's painting my portrait and he's nearly old enough to be my father.'

'And what difference has that ever made? I only hope he's painting you with your clothes on. Anyway, you need to remember that he's Lina's private perk and it doesn't do to upset Lina.'

'I had no idea. I thought he was supposed to be gay.'

'That's more than likely, but it doesn't stop him being Lina's property. There's a lot you don't know, or pretend you don't, about this place, Fran.'

Francine was silent for a while and when she spoke again she sounded unusually diffident. 'Do you have sex with Tom?'

Alice turned to her in astonishment. 'I've been married to the man for six years – what do you think we do?'

'And before you were married?'

'When we had the chance.'

'Your choice or his?'

Alice grinned. 'Let's say mutual attraction. But what's this leading up to?'

'I'll have to have it out with Paul. Now I've got the flat he'll be getting ideas, and I've no intention of going down that road.'

'You mean marriage?'

'Good God, no! I mean sex.'

Alice put down her little bed, still incomplete, and gave Francine her undivided attention. 'Are you saying that you've never had it off with Paul?'

'Nor with anybody else. It repels me.'

Alice was shaken. 'My God! *Virgo intacta* at twenty-six! What is this? Are you after some sort of record? . . . Paul isn't exactly my idea of a ball of fire but I can't help feeling sorry for the poor man.' She went on, 'It puzzles me what you see in men if you feel like that.'

'I don't know. It's a game I suppose. They're so damned smug . . . You feel you want to . . . I don't know—'

'To take them down a peg? Is that it? So you lead 'em up the garden and then it's "Back in your box, Bonzo" . . . If it's a game it's a dangerous one, Fran.'

'It's not like that.'

'Anyway, while we're on the subject of your sex life, or lack of it, are you still seeing much of Bob Lander?'

'He comes to the carving shop now and then for a gossip and I look in at the pottery.'

Alice resumed work on her bed. 'If you ask me, there's a thing between him and Emile. By the way, how do you get on with his keeper?'

'Oh, Derek's all right; I quite like him. Of course, he's extremely intelligent and Bob treats him like he was some sort of guru. It's a funny set-up but I like going there now and then, when I get bored.'

Alice said, 'Lina doesn't like to see anybody too friendly with Bob or Derek.'

'Any idea why?'

'Maybe she doesn't trust them. I don't know. It could be a policy of divide and rule. Anyway, Derek is a top-class potter and in a position to make his own arrangements, whatever Lina thinks.' Alice looked across at Francine. 'But where does all this leave Paul?'

Francine said, 'Paul is different. He's been around a long time and I'm used to him.' A frown. 'In a funny sort of way, I need him.' 'And that's all that matters. No wonder he goes about looking like a wet week. Is this sex thing something that happened to you while you were away?'

'When they locked me up, you mean. No, I don't think so, though the kind of sex that was on offer there didn't appeal to me either.'

Francine added after a break, 'You don't understand what it's like to be me, Alice.'

'Does that mean you'd rather be somebody else?'

Francine looked puzzled. 'Somebody else? I've never even thought about it. I'm quite content as I am.'

Alice was having trouble with the alignment of one of the joints and there was silence for a while, broken at last by a sudden sharp shower which drenched the windows and blotted out the moor.

When it was over Alice said, 'You spend a lot of time with Paul apart from working together – what do you do?'

'In the evenings we mostly play chess. He's good, and he's teaching me. I like it, and last week I beat him twice.' She broke off. 'Funny! You'd think he'd have been upset, but he seemed pleased.'

Alice sighed. 'Chess! . . . I don't know what to make of you, Fran. I only hope you know what you're doing.'

Another longish pause then Alice, hesitant, asked, 'Is it true what they're saying, that you've come into money?'

'Yes. From an aunt I scarcely knew, I suppose it's all around the site?'

'There's talk. What will you do?'

Francine smiled. 'I'm thinking of buying in here if I can get the right sort of deal from Lina.'

A few days later

In Emile Collis's studio Francine, wearing a floral dress, posed in an armchair. Sitting askew, an open book in her lap, she was apparently absorbed in what she read.

Half-length portrait of a young woman reading.

The painting carried its catalogue entry (if it ever got that far) like a label. As a portrait painter Collis was almost a century too late.

In a grubby paint-stained overall he worked at his easel. He was fortyish, lean and bony, with a mass of tiny black curls which contrasted oddly with his pale features.

'You've moved your head, Fran . . . Turn just a little more to the light and keep your eyes on the book.'

'I'm getting stiff, Emile.'

Collis dropped his brush into the pot. 'Yes, all right. We'll take a break.' He stood back from his easel. 'I can't get your profile. Damn it! I've drawn you often enough. I ought to be able to do this with my eyes shut, but just because this is bloody paint . . .'

Collis lived and worked in a long low building on the rising ground behind the Archers' house and his studio was sandwiched between his flat and the frame workshop. It was square and bare with three or four easels, a painter's trolley on castors, a stool or two and cupboards around the walls. The light was controlled by blinds. On two of the easels there were blocked-in canvases of beach scenes and propped on the edge of each was a photograph from which the picture could be developed. 'Beach and coastal scenes with figures' were Collis's staple contribution to the Guild.

Francine massaged her thighs.

'Feel like a coffee?'

'If you like.'

While Collis went to make the coffee Francine wandered into the framing shop. Collis framed all the Guild's pictures, arguing that a frame can make or break a picture.

The shop was equipped with a state-of-the-art mitring machine and a bench with a variety of clamps for gluing, while mouldings of all sorts and sizes were stacked in racks against a wall.

'Oh, you're in here. Coffee's ready.'

'Do you frame the pictures Lina buys in Amsterdam?'

Emile looked mildly put out. 'So you know about them.'

'Doesn't everybody?'

A small shrug. 'Possibly. I suppose they must do if you say so, but Lina likes to think not.'

'Why?'

'Perhaps she feels the Guild members wouldn't like her having a side-line.'

'Archer has his St Ives gallery.'

'Yes.'

'*Do* you frame the pictures she buys?'

Collis hesitated, then, 'No. She takes them to a little shop near the Oude Kerk in Amsterdam.'

'So they arrive framed?'

'Yes, but why the interest, Fran?'

'I just like to know.'

'Well, now you do, so come and have your coffee.'

She followed him back through the studio into his flat and the little kitchen–living room which was not unlike her own.

'Biscuit?'

Francine had not finished. 'You lived in Amsterdam for a time, didn't you?'

'Yes, but that wasn't where I met Lina and Archer.' Collis sat back in his chair. 'Look, Fran, let's get this straight. I think I know what it's all about. You've come into money and you're thinking of investing in the Guild.'

'Did Lina tell you that?'

'Yes.'

'You must be in her confidence.'

'I wouldn't say that, but I do want to say something to you. Think very carefully about what you're doing.'

'I always do.'

'Good! Now let's get back to painting.'

'Just one more question. You are gay, aren't you, Emile?'

He turned on her. 'What the hell is that to do with you?'

'I'd just like to know.'

'Yes, and one of these days you'll know too much. Have you been talking to Blond Bob?'

'Not about you.'

'Good! I'd like you to keep it that way. Now, are you going back to the pose or not?'

An hour later Collis put down his brush. 'It's no good! That's it for today, Fran.'

Francine got up from the chair and threw down the book. 'Do I put you off?'

'You're no help.'

'Marsden never complained when he painted me.'

'Perhaps you didn't talk so much.'

'Can I look?'

'No.'

'Do you want me tomorrow afternoon?'

'I don't know.'

'Suit yourself.'

After Francine had gone Collis covered his palette and was attending to his brushes when he had another visitor.

'Lina!'

Lina Archer was a well-built, muscular, vigorous woman in her late forties. She wore her assisted-blonde hair in a page-boy cut, her eyes were blue and cold. Lina Archer: a firm figure appropriate to her Dutch ancestry.

'You look flustered, Emile.'

Collis said nothing and Lina went on, 'I saw Francine leaving. Has she been getting at you?' Her English was perfect and colloquial; only her slightly gutteral delivery gave any clue to her origins.

'Just questions.'

'What sort of questions?' Lina was peremptory.

'Oh, about the pictures. Do they arrive framed, or do I frame them.'

'What did you tell her?'

Collis was silent and Lina demanded, 'I'm asking you what you told Francine.'

Collis's manner was that of a schoolboy caught out. 'I told her that you take them to a shop in the Oude Kerk.'

Lina's expression hardened. 'That was foolish.'

Collis said nothing and Lina went on, 'I want that girl with us, Emile. She could be very useful and not only through her money. She's the right sort, but she needs careful handling.'

Collis was sullen. 'I think she could be dangerous.'

'And so you hand her information which she would be better without at this stage.' A brief pause, then, 'Anyway, there's probably no harm done. I can manage that young woman.'

The Friday before Whitsun

The wood-carvers' workshop occupied the ground floor of a little two-storied building on the far side of the stream. Francine's flat, above the workshop, was reached by an outside stair at the back.

At half-past eight in the evening Francine was in her living room, awaiting the arrival of a visitor. She was restless, though she refused to admit that the prospect of the visit troubled her. She told herself more than once that she was fully briefed, that she held the cards and could make her own terms.

All the same, she had put on the floral dress which she wore for the painting, the only dress she had. And she was looking around her little room with a critical eye. Absurdly perhaps, she had even bought a bottle of sherry.

At shortly after half-past eight she saw Lina making her way over the bridge. Lina in trousers and woolly jumper, looking masculine. Francine thought, I've got it wrong. She waited while the woman walked round to the back of the house, climbed the stairs and knocked. Only then did she get up to let her in.

'Francine!' The tone, the manner – Lina always got it right. Now it said, I've come to talk to you and that is a concession in itself.

Despite the differences in age and experience, they were well matched.

In the living room Lina looked about her. 'You haven't changed anything much. Archer and I lived in this little flat for a few months while they were getting the house ready.' Then, with a disarming smile, 'I can see that you are not house proud.'

'Does that count for or against me?'

Lina was taken aback. 'I'm sorry! I assure you— '

'No need to apologise. You've come here, presumably, to make your assessment, as I shall make mine. I simply want to keep an eye on the score.'

Lina recovered sufficiently to smile. 'I can see that I shall have to watch my step.'

They sat on either side of a small table by the window and Lina got down to business. 'I understand that your legacy amounts to around fifty thousand pounds.'

'That is the amount I'm considering as an investment in the Guild.'

'Certainly that would allow us to expand. I have in mind metal-working of some kind – not the small-scale stuff – jewellery and such like. That wasn't a success when we tried it earlier. But there is a growing demand for high-quality ornamental ironwork. Of course, whatever we do we shall have to recruit one, or possibly two really good craftsmen.'

'Would that be difficult?'

'I'm not sure. What will be difficult is persuading Archer to accept the changes. I mean, the Guild will need to be reconstructed on different lines; lines that will conflict with the astrological model he had in mind from the start.' She smiled. 'But don't worry about that; I think I can handle it.'

Francine remembered her sherry. 'Would you care for a glass of sherry?'

'What? Oh, yes, that might be pleasant.'

The bottle and glasses were produced. 'Ah, fino!' Lina approved.

Francine poured the sherry. 'I'm sorry I've no jenever. Isn't that what you call it?' Francine being mischievous.

'I do not drink gin!' Lina said, with emphasis. She raised her glass. 'To the Guild and its future!'

The toast drunk, Lina got back to business. 'I assume that you fully understand the present Guild set-up.'

'I'm not sure that I do.'

Raised eyebrows. 'But surely! You've been a Guild member for a long time and recently, from what I hear, you have made it your business to sound out other members – filling in matters of detail, I suppose.' Lina added with her thin-lipped smile, 'To the annoyance of some of them, I believe. But let me run over the facts, if only to remind you. Members of the Guild rent their premises and equipment from us— '

Francine interrupted. ' "Us" being the management – you and Archer.'

A moment of hesitation. 'If you wish to put it like that.'

'But that is how it is, and if I invest in the Guild I shall want to join the management on terms according to my investment.'

Lina sipped her sherry and replaced her glass on the table. 'I see that you have it all worked out. But going back to our present organisation, as I was about to say, we obtain the orders on terms agreed by the members— '

Again Francine interrupted. 'I understand that, but there is a condition which says that members are not allowed to do business except through the Guild.'

A broad gesture. 'But surely that is a reasonable, indeed an inevitable condition in the circumstances.'

'Perhaps, but you and Archer, though members, are not apparently bound by it.'

A pause, and a cold stare. 'I suppose you are referring to Archer's gallery in St Ives. But that is a quite separate undertaking pre-dating the formation of the Guild, and Archer— '

Francine cut her short. 'But there is also the matter of your dealings in imported pictures from Amsterdam, and with the little shop near the Oude Kerk. Are these also quite separate under-takings?'

Francine's shots seemed to find a target. Lina paused with her sherry glass halfway to her lips. She was flushed. 'You have been listening to gossip, Francine! I cannot believe that you could see these arrangements as contrary— '

Having effectively rocked the boat Francine felt she could afford to offer some reassurance. 'There is no need to get heated, Lina. I'm not out to make difficulties. Far from it. But if I am to join you and Archer in the management of the Guild I shall want all aspects of the business taken into account. I shall want to know exactly what is going on.'

Lina was disturbed, her manner less confident. 'You realise that I shall have to discuss all aspects of this with Archer. I have no doubt that we shall be able to work out some sort of agreement but my main problem will still be to overcome his objections to changing the structure of the Guild to which he attaches so much importance.'

She stood up. 'I hope that we shall talk again.'

Francine said, 'I've just one more question.'

'Indeed?'

'What exactly is the position of Blond Bob?'

Lina seemed surprised by this. 'Bob Lander is at present Derek Scawn's assistant in the pottery. There is, as you know, a vacancy in the Guild and Derek would like to see Bob filling that place. Why do you ask?'

Francine was casual. 'No special reason. I just had the impression from talking to him that there was more to it than that.'

'Yes. Well, Bob tries very hard to make himself interesting.'

Lina waited for some response and when none came she seemed put out. 'At least we've broken the ice and, as I said, I shall talk to Archer. I hope that in the meantime— '

'In the meantime I have nothing to say to anyone.'

Lina nodded. 'That is good. We shall talk again.' And she left, significantly less assured than on her arrival.

After she had gone Francine sprawled on the tatty armchair, looking at the two glasses and the sherry bottle on a table by the window. She got up, poured herself half a glass and drank it off. She was unused to alcohol and it went to her head. She felt elevated.

She had started something.

Usually she thought little about her future, and when she did her thoughts were vague, but Lina's visit had changed everything. Now there was the prospect of getting involved with the Guild on terms that would give her real authority. Coping with Lina would be a challenge but she looked forward to that.

A totally new way of life. And she was intrigued to think where it might lead. But no sex, and certainly no marriage. Smiling to herself, she recalled the nativity play all those years ago, when a newspaper had dubbed her 'The Quiet Virgin'. She decided to settle for that.

Restless, she wondered about going for a walk but dusk was closing over the moor and she finally decided on bed.

She got up from her chair and went through to the little bedroom at the back of the house. Twin beds: one made up, the other tumbled as she had left it that morning. Her black-faced doll lay neglected on the pillow. She undressed, got into bed and pulled the clothes over them both.

Wrapped in a shawl, Blackie had been a stand-in for baby Jesus in the nativity play. Later, when she was arrested, she had been allowed to keep him with her. Later still, at the cost of a litany of dirty jokes, she had held on to him through three years in the Young Offenders.

Now, in the near darkness, lying on her back and staring up at the ceiling she told herself that she and Lina had much in common. *Lina's my sort; too much so perhaps.* She even wondered if there would be room for the two of them.

And a little later she was thinking; *Lina's got Archer and I've got Paul . . .*

She turned on her side and cuddled down with the doll in her arms. 'Never mind, Blackie! You'll always be here.'

And then, 'Poor Archer . . . Poor Paul!'

That same evening
Archer was sitting at his table by the window, surrounded by his books and his manuscript records. Star charts were Blu-tacked to the walls and there was a single bed tucked away, as far as that was possible, behind the door.

With his greying silky hair and beard, meticulously trimmed, he looked like some Victorian icon, a Tennyson, or a Darwin after a visit to the barber.

From his window he had a view of the moor stretching away to the cliffs and the sea. The sky was darkening, and though there was still the remnant of an orange flush away to the west, he could already see the flashing signal from Godrevy light.

With no wind, the silence was total.

Depressed, resentful and unable to settle to his work, he listened for his wife's return. She had not even told him where she was going; but he knew.

At last he heard the sound of her key in the front door and minutes later, her footsteps on the stairs.

'So there you are!'

Where else had she expected to find him?

She came into the room looking flushed. Archer braced himself. Although she owed him an apology for going behind his back he knew he would soon be under attack.

'I've been talking to Francine.'

'I know.'

Lina switched on the light and sat herself on the end of the bed. 'Someone had to talk to her.'

Archer gathered together the bones of his argument. 'That girl is trouble, Lina. She's a Scorpio and she should never have been admitted to the Guild. I was against it from the start.'

Pleased with this firm opening, he fondled his beard and went on, 'Of course, there's nothing we can do about that now, but we can— '

Lina cut in. 'We would have lost Paul if we hadn't admitted her. They work well together and, in any case, she is more than paying her own way.'

Archer shuffled the papers in front of him. 'All I'm saying is that we mustn't allow her to get any further. If she puts the money from her wretched legacy into the Guild she will be a partner with us.' He shifted his chair so that he faced his wife. 'And you know what Scorpios are: once they move into any situation they are never content until they dominate it.'

Lina smiled. 'But you must know by now, Archer, that I am not easily dominated.'

Archer gestured irritably. 'No, but that doesn't reassure me. My idea when I started the Guild was that it should be an opportunity for fruitful co-operation between nine like-minded crafts people. Not a battlefield . . . That girl would destroy everything that I value in the Guild.' A brief pause before, greatly daring, he added, 'And sometimes I think that is what you want.'

Lina was mild. 'No, that is unfair. I don't want to destroy anything, but in business there is no standing still. You either grow or you go under, and in order to grow we need capital.'

'So you tell me, but I have never heard any convincing reason why a steady turn-over cannot be maintained.' Archer turned back to his table. 'We shall never agree on this, Lina . . . Never!'

There was a lull. Archer went through the pretence of resuming work while Lina sat and waited, knowing there was more to come.

It was longer in coming than she had expected and she was on the point of leaving when Archer turned to face her once more.

'There's another thing that worries me about that girl. It seems that she is upsetting the others by going around asking questions.'

Lina was guarded. 'I suppose it's natural that she should want to know exactly what she would be putting her money into, and what the attitudes of the others would be.'

Archer was dismissive. 'There's more to it than that, as I think you must know. Emile is certainly not himself and hasn't been since he's been seeing so much of that girl.'

'He's painting her portrait. Has he said anything to you?'

'Not directly.' Archer made a vague gesture. 'There's something going on and the girl is stirring it up. It's not only Emile . . . There's Lander . . . I can't put it into words but there's a general sort of unease— ' He broke off. 'You're quite sure you don't know what it's all about?'

'If you want my honest opinion, I think you're imagining it.'

Once more Archer turned back to his table. 'In that case there's no more to be said.'

Lina stood up. 'Well, nothing has been agreed with Francine. It was just a preliminary talk, and I am very tired. The girl is not as discreet as she might be and no doubt there will be problems. All I am saying is that her money would make a great deal of difference to our prospects and the possibility of an arrangement is worth considering.'

Archer was about to reply but Lina was gone and her 'Good-night' came from across the passage.

Chapter Two

Whit-Saturday evening

The Wycliffes had finished their meal and cleared away. Helen was reading a novel, Wycliffe turned the pages of the *Western Morning News*.

The room looked out on a garden bounded by trees through which they could glimpse the waters of the estuary. It was growing dusky but neither of them had got up to switch on the lights.

A photograph and a minor headline caught Wycliffe's attention. 'There's a piece here about Paul Bateman. He's made a name for himself as a wood-carver and he's done a frieze for one of the National Trust houses.'

Helen said, 'Remind me.'

'That Christmas, ten years ago. You were staying with David in Kenya, when Jack was born— '

'And you spent Christmas with the Bishops at that weird house with a funny name on the cliff near Zennor. That girl shot her father. Wasn't he an MP or something?'

'Mynhager, that was the house. Yes, Gerald Bateman. Paul was his son and the girl who shot him was his natural daughter.'

Helen said, 'What happened to the girl? I remember that she had a French name and that you were very impressed by her.'

'Francine Lemarque. She was sixteen and they sent her to a Young Offenders. I felt badly about it but I did nothing . . . Bateman was a bastard and deserved what he got. I often wonder what happened to Francine. She was a strange girl. A few nights before the shooting she gave a little gem of a performance as the Virgin in the church nativity play.* I intended to keep in touch.'

Helen said, 'Cheer up! It's Saturday. We've got the Whit weekend in front of us and it could even be fine.'

'And on Tuesday I've got to face the new chief. Just our luck to be among the first forces in the country to be saddled with a woman CC.'

'Does it worry you?'

'No. As King Louis said of a new Pope, "If he doesn't suit I shall take a course with him."'

'Sounds virile. What would you do?'

'Apply for my pension.'

'Let's go to bed.'

That same evening

Once more Francine was looking out of her window, expecting a visitor. She saw Paul crossing the stream. Tall and slim and dark and tentative. Paul always looked where he was going and thought about what he would say.

Francine told herself, 'He's nice. Like a tabby cat who purrs when he's stroked. If only he would bite . . . '

She waited. Paul looked up, saw her and waved. She heard him on the stairs. She had told him not to knock and a moment later he was in the room, standing, questioning.

Francine did nothing to help him and finally he said, 'What shall we do?'

'I don't mind.'

Another interval. 'What about a game?' He was looking at the chessboard.

'If you like.'

They sat at the little table by the window; the chessboard was set up and Paul said, 'White to open.'

Francine, preoccupied, made her move without interest: 'Pawn to K4.'

* *Wycliffe and the Quiet Virgin*

They used the old notation because that was how Paul had been taught.

He responded. 'Pawn to K4.'

Francine hesitated, then, 'Knight to KB3.'

From Paul, after consideration. 'Pawn to Q3.'

Several moves later Paul said, 'You don't want to go on with this, do you?'

'No. We need to talk.'

'About us?'

'Yes.'

'Is there anything new to say?'

'There is. I've made up my mind about one thing. We can never live together as a couple, Paul. I'm sorry.'

'You mean that you will never have sex with me.'

'Yes, that is what I mean.'

'Because we have the same father?'

Francine hesitated, then decided to cheat. 'Yes.'

Paul sighed and was silent for a long time, then, 'Well, if that's how it must be I can live with it. One day you may change your mind and as long as we carry on working and sharing as we do, I shan't complain. I want to be with you, Fran; that's what matters.'

It was Francine's turn to be silent and now, deeply worried, Paul asked, 'Is there someone else? Is what they're saying true?'

'There is no one else.'

'Then we carry on as now.'

'We carry on working together.'

'And outside of work?'

'No, Paul. I don't think so.'

'But— '

'Listen. We are two quite different people. We happen to have been thrown together for a few years when we were young and impressionable, but in the things that matter we have nothing in common. I killed a man, Paul – your father and mine— '

'I have never blamed you for that. I have never held it against you. That man destroyed the only family you knew.'

Francine played with her queen, rolling the little piece between finger and thumb. 'You've been good to me, Paul; and understanding, beyond anything I could expect. I owe you everything.' She paused. 'But I'm not the sort to pay my debts. We are different; we want different things. You want stability – security – I want to live life near the edge, and I want to start before I'm too old to handle it.'

Paul sat for a little while in silence, then with many hesitations he said, 'You've been going around asking a lot of questions about the running of the Guild and now you are getting involved with Lina . . . Do you think that is the way to get the best out of your life here?'

It was the first time Paul had even come near to criticising her and it was an odd experience. She said, 'I am not getting involved as you say. I intend to find out what is going on first, then I shall decide what I want to do about it.'

There was another long silence then, in a choking voice, Paul said, 'I can't talk any more now, but I'm not going to give up.' In a vigorous movement he got to his feet, catching a corner of the chessboard so that several pieces rolled off on the floor, and he was gone.

Francine remained seated for a while. The low sun was shining in at the window and she realised that she was uncomfortably warm and sticky. The exchange with Paul was inevitable but it had been disturbing. She went into the kitchen, saw the bottle of sherry on the shelf, and drank straight from it. She decided to have a bath.

In the bedroom she undressed, put on her dressing-gown and went into the little bathroom where there was scarcely space to move around. She turned on the taps to provide the blend of hot and cold that she preferred and waited. For the first time, she realised she was sleepy. The sherry?

She sat on the bath stool and felt increasingly drowsy. The bath was filling and she watched through a haze of uncertainty. She had a headache. The bath seemed to be over-filling.

She couldn't face it. She reached for the taps and turned them off, then staggered back to the bedroom, supporting herself briefly against the doorpost. She reached the bed, pulled back the clothes, and fell into bed. Blackie rolled over the edge on to the floor.

Whit-Sunday morning

Mulfra Cove lay open to its vast horizon: the sun shone fitfully out of a broken sky and cloud shadows darkened the face of the sea. Out there one had only to follow the great circle and it was next stop Newfoundland.

Closer to hand were the tumbled boulders and weed-strewn sands of the cove. There was no wind, but a slow swell broke along the shore with a curious ripping sound like the tearing of linen.

The cove was bounded by two promontories and halfway down the nearer one Mynhager, home of the Bishop family, clung to its ledge, almost as rugged and ragged as the cliff itself. Mynhager translates with an Arthurian flavour into 'edge perilous'; a mad place to build anything, but the house had been there for more than a century.

It was breakfast time for the remnants of the Bishop family – the two sisters, Caroline and Virginia. Paul was not with them.

Both women were in their late forties. For years now they had taken their meals in the kitchen, where tall cupboards, a giant stoneware sink and a massive central table bedded uncomfortably with a chest freezer, a microwave and a fan-assisted oven.

Virginia had in front of her a bowl of milky bran-flakes without sugar. She ate absent-mindedly, her attention on yesterday's *Telegraph*, folded beside her plate.

Caroline ate her toast, spread with butter and marmalade. Caroline had always been plump, now she was becoming fat. She was thinking of Paul, and how she had never quite got used to being a mother, but she worried about him . . .

Virginia finished her bran-flakes and lit a cigarette. Caroline started to clear the table and Virginia spread her newspaper over the available space.

Caroline said, 'Paul didn't come home last night. That's two nights running.'

'So he stayed at the craft centre. He's done it before.'

'I'm afraid that now Francine's got the flat there he'll move in with her.'

Virginia turned the pages of her newspaper. 'I suppose he might. They call it sex.'

Caroline stopped on her way to the sink with a handful of cutlery. 'It's easy to see you haven't got a child of your own, Vee.'

'No, that's one blessing I've escaped. Thanks be! But if Paul is sleeping with Francine there's not much you can do about it. He's twenty-seven, for God's sake.'

'I'm still his mother.'

'But that's not what's worrying you, is it? Your problem is who his father was.'

Caroline pouted. 'You can be very hurtful when you want to be, Vee.'

'Yes. Well, if you remember, we agreed all those years ago that to survive we had to face reality, but we're still not very good at it.'

Virginia had started on the crossword. Caroline dropped the cutlery into the washing-up bowl with a clatter.

The door bell clanged, sounding like a signal to lower the drawbridge.

Caroline said, 'There's someone at the door,' and went to answer it.

Virginia was aware of a mild commotion before Caroline returned, flustered. 'It's the police; there's two of them. I've taken them into the drawing room. It's about Francine— '

'What about Francine?'

'She's dead . . . They think she's been murdered.'

That same Whit-Sunday morning in the Wycliffes' garden

A late spring morning in the garden of the Watch House and Wycliffe felt that momentarily he was as near to perfect contentment as he was ever likely to get. His book had slipped from his fingers on to the grass, his eyes were almost, though not completely, closed and he was seeing the world through a vaguely distorting fluid opalescence. Helen, busy with her weeding, seemed insubstantial, and her actions improbable. At the slightest movement of his lids even the estuary changed its configuration: trees became taller and more slender, or shrank and spread their branches. He was in control.

In his enjoyment of the moment, in the very background of his mind he was aware of only one tiny flaw. It was Sunday – and Whit Sunday at that. His progenitors on both sides had been dyed-in-the-wool Methodists. Of course he had given up trying to emulate the Red Queen in believing six impossible things before breakfast, and he sometimes wondered if there could be a religion without magic, and without fear. But being dyed-in-the-wool still meant something and so, in a mildly disturbing fashion, did Whit Sunday.

Then he opened his eyes wide and in an instant he was back in the real world, a much more complex and disturbing world where there were decisions to be made; one in particular.

Bertram Oldroyd, his chief, had finally retired and his successor had been appointed. A woman. To say that the appointment had surprised everybody was an understatement. Even Oldroyd, obviously the first to hear, resorted to the vernacular and admitted to being gobsmacked. But whatever they thought or said, the new chief was a woman: Jane Elizabeth Sawle LLB, formerly deputy chief of Severn Valley.

Wycliffe, along with his colleagues, had already met her in a socialising get-to-know-you session, with drinks and party morsels. A pleasant enough woman, late forties, dignified but not starchy. Word had it that the Home Office had her in their sights for the Inspectorate and that this was a stepping stone.

The question was Stay? Or Go? And for once Helen had been no help. 'Just ask yourself if you can do without it.' The very question he could not answer.

Then his mobile put an end to both enjoyment and introspection. Even Macavity, the Wycliffe cat, opened a disapproving eye.

'Wycliffe!' Fiercely.

As it happened, the duty officer in CID was DS Lucy Lane.

'We have a suspected homicide in the St Ives area, sir. This morning a young woman was found dead in her flat above one of the craft workshops belonging to an outfit that calls itself the Guild of Nine. The police surgeon has diagnosed carbon-monoxide poisoning, resulting from a blockage in the vent from a gas water-heater. And DI Prisk is satisfied that the blockage was deliberately contrived.'

'Where exactly is this Guild place?'

'On the moor, close to the village of Mulfra, a few miles along the coast road from St Ives.'

St Ives, Mulfra, a craft workshop . . . It was uncanny . . . Paul Bateman, Francine Lemarque . . . No, it was too absurd!

He didn't ask the name of the dead girl. In any case, it was quite likely that Lucy would not have known it.

But the names alone were enough to open a Pandora's box of memories. He listened to what more Lucy had to tell him, then he called DI Kersey.

'I'm afraid the weekend's over, Doug. I'll give you what details I've got, then I want you to notify SOCO and follow me down with a small team. It's Lucy's Sunday on so I'll get her to pick me up.'

For several years Lucy Lane had worked with him on all his major cases and she had consistently refused promotion. It happened that their temperaments, even their prejudices, dove-tailed, so that they functioned naturally as a team. At one time there had been gossip, but it had long since talked itself out.

Helen suspended her weeding and came towards him, sweeping her hair back with a bare arm because her hands were earthy. Now there were traces of grey in that hair but the gesture was exactly as he remembered it from the days when they were a newly married couple and he was a beat copper in the Midlands.

'Something cropped up?'

'A suspected homicide near St Ives.' He did not mention Mulfra. 'Lucy is coming to fetch me.'

Matter-of-fact. Just another case; a crisis in the lives of total strangers.

While waiting for Lucy he telephoned Dr Franks, the pathologist, and was lucky to find him at home. Franks was almost certainly bored for his manner was breezy and forthcoming. 'Well, Charles, what have you got for me?'

And, as usual, this breeziness provoked a sour response from Wycliffe. 'A homicide, apparently. What were you expecting?'

Helen had packed his bag and he added something to read in bed. He changed into a workaday suit. Lucy came to pick him up, and it was still short of midday when they arrived in that cradle of Cornishness called Penwith. The name translates as 'the end of the end', which may seem needlessly repetitive, but being there for a while brings enlightenment to the perceptive.

They drove to St Ives and out by the coast road which follows the margin of the granite moor where it meets the slaty rocks of the coastal plain.

A sharp shower, then the sun shone again. Wycliffe recalled vividly that earlier time when he was driving alone to spend Christmas with the Bishops at Mynhager.

They arrived in the former mining village of Mulfra, with its stark little church, its chapel, its 'Men's Institute', its pub and its cottages, all strung out along the road, sprawling only a little towards the sea on the one hand and into the moor on the other.

Wycliffe knew the village well. Ten years ago he had even stayed for a few nights at the Tributers', a pub which had survived the collapse of mining by catering for those odd enough to want to live there, and for visitors wishing to see something of the real Cornwall.

Lucy said, 'Here we are!' A uniformed constable was stationed at the entrance to a track leading up into the moor.

'It's about a quarter of a mile, sir, and the track is quite passable. DI Prisk is in charge and he's there with the police surgeon.'

Two or three cottages with little other sign of life, but all around, buried for the most part, the artefacts of people who had lived and worked on this land through six or seven thousand years; with some of their bones – not many, for bones succumb to the acid soil and, in any case, cremation was fashionable for much of the time.

The track divided, a fact not mentioned by the guardian copper, but a woman from one of the cottages was hanging out her washing with a wary eye on the sky. She removed a peg from between her teeth. 'You keep right. What's happening? Is it some idiot who's fallen down a shaft?'

They were climbing gently on a winding track bordered by clumps of gorse in full bloom, golden and blatant.

In fact, the track soon divided again with a made-up road off to their right and a large well-painted sign: 'The Archer Guild of Nine' with a logo in the form of a stylised bow and arrow.

Lucy said, 'How subtle can you get?'

The path they were leaving was marked by an improvised fingerpost: 'To Nirvana'.

'They must have some odd ones around here.' Lucy again. Wycliffe had scarcely spoken a word throughout the trip.

They followed the made-up road into a shallow valley with scattered buildings. A water course divided the site, and the centre of interest was on the other side. Several vehicles were parked near the smallest of three buildings, of which they could see only the gable end. Lucy said, 'The bridge doesn't look much, but I suppose if they got over, we can.'

They did, and Lucy parked in line. A waiting uniformed man said, 'Around the back, sir.'

The building was two-storied and the steps led up to a little wooden balcony which ran around the corner of the house.

They had been spotted and DI Prisk appeared on the balcony. 'Up here, sir.'

Prisk was new to the job and for some reason Wycliffe found difficulty in taking him seriously. Perhaps it was a remark made by a member of the promotions board which dogged the poor man: 'He may be a good copper but he looks like a bloody rabbit.'

It was too true: the prominent incisors, the pinched cheeks and large pointed ears combined to make the image indelible.

At the top of the steps a door with glass panes stood open to a short passage. 'The room on the right, sir.'

It was a bedroom and Wycliffe took in the scene from the

doorway. Twin beds; and the body of the girl was sprawled on one of them, only partly covered by a dressing-gown.

Wycliffe looked down at her and muttered to himself, 'I knew it!'

The other bed was made up and undisturbed. By the window a portable electric fire burned, creating an intolerable stuffiness.

The police surgeon came up the passage to join him. 'In the circumstances I thought I'd better wait.'

Prisk said, 'Dr Forbes . . . Superintendent Wycliffe.'

Forbes was new and young, and sure of himself. Nobody's push-over. If you stay in a job long enough everybody else is new or young, or both.

'Not much I can say. She died of anoxia resulting from carbon-monoxide poisoning. You can see the characteristic patchy, reddish flush.'

Prisk added, 'And, as you'll see directly, the flue was deliberately blocked.'

Wycliffe was forcing himself to really look at the body on the bed. He saw the pale skin with the tell-tale patches, he saw the face in profile, partly obscured by the red-gold hair. It was one of the strangest and most disturbing moments in his experience.

So far he had not spoken a word to the others since entering the bedroom, nor had he acknowledged what he had been told.

Now he said in a colourless voice, 'This is Francine Lemarque.'

Prisk was at his side. 'You knew her, sir?' Prisk was clearly puzzled, first by his silence, now by his manner.

'Yes, I knew her. But what's she doing here?'

It was a silly question but Prisk did his best. 'It seems she worked for the Guild of Nine in the wood-carving shop downstairs. She'd been with them for a couple of years but she moved into this flat only a few weeks ago.'

Wood-carving . . .

Wycliffe was struggling to match this present with the remembered past.

So Paul and Francine had remained together. Rather, they had come together again after Francine had served her sentence . . . And now . . . ?

He continued to look at the body as though mesmerised. The face, seen in profile, was untouched except for that flush, but the eyes were staring.

Deeply moved, he controlled himself and set about the routine questions.

'Who found her?'

'The chap she worked with called Bateman – Paul Bateman. He's downstairs in the workshop and he seems devastated.'

Wycliffe saw in his mind's eye the lean, shy youth who had followed Francine around like a loyal but unwanted dog.

'Does he live on the site?'

'No, he lives with his people in the house down by the cove.'

'Mynhager.'

Prisk looked at him oddly. 'Yes. I understand the girl lived there too until a few weeks ago, when she moved into this flat.'

Wycliffe struggled to keep his mind on the present. He turned to the doctor. 'Anything to say on time of death?'

Forbes pondered. 'Last night. My guess is that she's been dead between twelve and sixteen hours, but Franks may have other ideas. That electric fire has retarded rigor but accelerated putrefaction.'

Wycliffe snapped, 'Yes, turn the damn thing off!'

Prisk was getting restless. 'I think you should see the cause of all this, sir.'

On the other side of the passage there was a tiny bathroom and the bath was two-thirds full of water.

Prisk pointed to a gas water-heater on the wall. 'There's a gas tank that supplies the buildings on this side of the stream and that heater is the culprit. The vent has been deliberately blocked. You can see it from the balcony.'

Wycliffe followed him outside and around the corner of the balcony. Prisk pointed to a standard square louvred vent, secured to the wall next to the little window of the bathroom and within easy reach. What looked like a bath towel had been wound around the vent and pressed in tightly, effectively blocking the louvres on all sides.

Prisk said, 'Ingenious, don't you think?'

Ingenious. Wycliffe saw it differently. As the manifestation of a cold festering hatred which he had never experienced and would never understand.

Back in the flat Forbes was ready to bow out. 'Well, if that's all, I'll be off. The rest is up to Franks. This was supposed to be my free Sunday. I'll let you have my report.'

Fox, the long, lanky Scene-of-Crime officer, turned up with, among other things, his assistant. Fox's unfortunate assistant was treated like a beast of burden.

With his camera Fox made a preliminary survey, clicking and picking his way around like a discriminating stork.

Wycliffe was still trapped in a limbo between past and present. Instant memories recalled in scenes and phrases that surfaced for a moment and were gone. Francine in the chancel of the village church, wearing a blue gown and caught in the spotlight, singing a lullaby – the Virgin in a nativity play. Francine at Mynhager, leafing through an album of old photographs, pondering over them – intent, lost.

Francine, at the top of the stairs, a gun in her hand, standing over a body which lay in a pool of blood: the body of Gerald Bateman MP, her natural father.

Now Fox was saying, 'You'd think she was too old for this sort of thing.' He had picked up a black-faced doll from the floor and dropped it on the bed.

Wycliffe recalled DI Kersey's words after Francine's arrest. 'She insisted on taking her black doll with her.'

Lucy Lane had disappeared. It was part of their routine. She would take a general look around, mingle and gossip where occasion arose, and come back with some lively titbits.

Wycliffe turned to Prisk. 'Let's get out of here.'

They went to stand on the little balcony. 'Have you contacted the relatives?'

'Yes. As soon as we had an ID my sergeant and a WPC went to Mynhager, where she lived before she came here. I asked Paul Bateman to break the news, to go with them, but he wouldn't. It seems they're not exactly relatives but they're all she's got around here, at any rate.'

Wycliffe, reflective, said, 'Yes, the Bishop family. She wasn't related to them in the ordinary sense, but they had good reason to take her in.'

Prisk looked at him. 'You really do know this young woman, sir. Anyway, according to my chap their reaction was odd; not indifferent exactly, but cautious.'

Wycliffe could believe that. 'Presumably they asked about Paul?'

'Yes, and our man explained the situation.'

'Right! Now, what about the set-up here, this craft colony or whatever it is?'

'I can't tell you much, sir. It was started before my time by a chap called Archer, who still runs it. He leased the old mine buildings and spent a packet on renovation and conversion. God knows how he got it through Planning.'

'Know anything about him?'

'I met him once in connection with a break-in at his gallery in St Ives. Seems a decent bloke. Arty type from way back. He's got a wife, but I've never met her. They say she's a foreigner – Dutch, I believe.'

'Any gossip about the place?'

Prisk pouted. 'Not much. The locals don't like the set-up on their doorstep but there's nothing you could pin down.'

Lucy joined them and Wycliffe asked, 'What's your impression?'

SOCO and Forensic would go over the flat with the proverbial fine-tooth comb. (Odd analogy – this device for combing out head lice). Anyway, their reports would run to pages of typescript, but it was from Lucy that he would learn how the place had been lived in.

'She wasn't house proud. The loo and the kitchen sink could do with some of that magic stuff that kills all known germs. And the vacuum cleaner could do with an outing. There's a locked desk in the kitchen–living room. It's a toy lock but I suppose we'd better leave that to Fox.. A radio but no TV. A fair number of books, mostly paperbacks by female authors. Austen to Woolf,

Mansfield and Murdoch. She must have had something in that head of hers.

'One other thing. It looks as though she had company last evening. On a table by the window there's a chessboard, apparently set up for play but it seems there might have been a quarrel; the pieces have been upset and there are some on the floor.'

They were interrupted by Franks, ready to add his special blend of wisdom, whimsy and wit in a recipe that was guaranteed to raise Wycliffe's hackles.

At the bottom of the steps he was already complaining. 'Well, Charles, it's a holiday weekend so I suppose you had to find something to keep yourself occupied.'

He climbed the steps, followed by his secretary. The pathologist's secretaries came and went. To date they had all been young and nubile; this one was matronly, a pleasant-looking woman in her forties. Perhaps at last his tastes were maturing to match his age.

'This is Viv. I don't think you've met her.'

A moment or two later he was bending over the body on the bed. 'Oh dear! What a waste! . . . Well, let's see what we can make of her.'

Viv stood by him, making selective notes from a flood of words. 'Anoxia as a result of CO poisoning . . . Otherwise, a healthy young woman . . . A virgin, incidentally. You'd have thought she'd have done something about that. She couldn't have been short of offers . . . Now, how did she get like this? Accident? Or some foul deed?' He turned to Wycliffe. 'Is that still a question?'

Wycliffe controlled himself. 'Apparently not.' He showed Franks the bathroom, the heater and the outside vent with its draped towel. 'Does that make sense?'

'As murder – yes. She would have undressed, put on her dressing-gown, gone into the bathroom and fussed about as women do, while she ran her bath.'

'Wouldn't she have noticed the fumes from the heater?'

'Probably not. The haemoglobin of our red cells, Charles, has a greater affinity for carbon monoxide than for oxygen and will pick it up from very low concentrations in the air we breathe.'

'Blocking the oxygen uptake.' Wycliffe disliked being spoon-fed, especially by Franks.

'Exactly, Charles! You're learning. The girl would feel a bit dizzy, she might have developed a sudden headache. Enough anyway to make her give up the idea of a bath. Obviously she turned off the water and went back to the bedroom.' Franks spread his hands. 'But too late. It's the classic pattern.'

'We've no way of knowing when the vent was blocked.'

'Your problem, Charles.'

'How long has she been dead?' Wycliffe pointed to the electric fire. 'Remember, that thing was on when our people got here and for some time afterwards.'

'I thought there was something. So all I've really got to go on is my crystal ball. What do you expect me to say? All right, let's make it latish yesterday evening and it's unlikely that I shall be able to improve on that.'

'Anything else?'

'Not until I've had her on the table. Now, if you'll get her to the mortuary SAP I might still get tomorrow off. I'll be in touch.'

He turned to his secretary. 'Right, Viv. We're away.'

Wycliffe walked with Franks to his car. The secretary went ahead and Franks watched her with an expression which could only be described as rueful. 'How's Helen?'

'Fine.'

'You're lucky, Charles. You got all this over early.'

'I'm no good at cryptic crosswords but is that a way of telling me that you're thinking of marriage?'

'What else is there at my age?'

'She seems a nice woman and she needs to be if she's going to put up with you.'

Franks said nothing for a while, then, 'She doesn't talk much, which is something . . . By the way, I'd like you and Helen to come to the wedding. Register Office of course. No flowers by request.'

'We'd like to come. When is it?'

Franks looked at him in astonishment. 'God! Don't rush me, Charles. I haven't asked her yet.'

As he was getting into his car, he turned. 'You look miserable, Charles. Just remember that every silver lining has a dirty great cloud behind it. So cheer up.'

A moment later the Porsche departed in a gravel-scattering screech of tyres. For years Franks had got away with driving like a lunatic and sleeping with his secretaries; for so long Wycliffe had come to the conclusion that there must be a department up there with the sole responsibility of looking after the Frankses of this world.

Kersey arrived. 'I've got Shaw, Dixon and Thorn with me but Potter and Curnow are on call if and when we need them. You said a small team.'

Wycliffe disliked having people around until the organisation was there to use them. A brief consultation with Prisk and it was agreed to set up an Incident Room in the Penzance nick where communications were good.

'Leave that to Prisk and Shaw. We shall need a caravan on the site. Get that organised and we'll have a briefing in the morning and get down to a routine. I want to clear my own mind before I start confusing other people's.'

The mortuary men arrived and carried the body away on a stretcher, enveloped in a plastic shroud. They had problems with the stairs but eventually they reached the waiting van and what remained of Francine Lemarque was driven away to the mortuary; there to suffer indignities that would do her no good at all but might help to discover who had killed her and so make everybody feel a bit better and a little safer.

At least there were no sightseers. In fact, the residents were being singularly discreet. And no media interest so far. A lot can happen on a Sunday, especially during a holiday weekend, before their instincts are aroused.

The body gone, it was possible to take a look at the bedroom. Lucy pointed to a framed drawing hanging above the bed head. It was in pencil, a head and shoulders of Francine, and it was the work of a natural.

It was inscribed, 'With love, Emile.'

Lucy said, 'I wonder who he is.'

'At any rate he can draw. Interesting.'

Wycliffe was striving to clear his mind, to be objective and professional. 'We believe that Francine died in the late evening or early in the night. Of course the vent must have been obstructed at some time before then, but it's visible from several places on the site. The obstruction itself wouldn't be noticed but anyone putting it there in daylight would be taking a risk.'

'So the inference is that the vent was blocked the night before.'

'They wouldn't know when she would take a bath.'

'But would that matter?' Anyway, let's go down and talk to the boy.'

He still thought of the twenty-seven-year-old Paul Bateman as 'the boy'.

Wycliffe was going through a very strange experience; it was like opening a book he had never read only to find that he had an intimate knowledge of some of the characters.

In the workshop downstairs Paul was seated on a work-bench by the window, legs dangling, surrounded by the tools of his craft. A young WPC sat on the only chair, prim and band-box neat.

She shook her head and murmured, 'Nothing, sir. Not a word.'

When she had gone Wycliffe said, 'You remember me, Paul?'

'Yes.'

On one of the benches there were several carved female figures in a similar stage of completion, and standing against one wall was the section of that frieze which he had seen in the newspaper photograph: an intricate design of fruit and flowers.

Wycliffe said, 'Perhaps we should move to somewhere we can talk.'

'I'm all right here.'

'I understand your distress, Paul, but we have to find out who did this to Francine.'

'Yes.'

'When did you last see her – alive?'

'Yesterday evening.' Paul had never been much given to speech;

a born craftsman, he expressed himself through the work of his hands and he was inept with words.

'You were playing chess?'

'Yes, we had started to play but Fran wanted to talk.'

'What about? Anything in particular?'

He hesitated. 'I don't know exactly. She wanted to change things, not to be together so much.'

'She wanted to stop working with you?'

Paul looked vaguely around the carving shop. 'No, I don't think it was that.' A pause, then, 'She didn't want anything beyond that.' His voice broke and there were tears in his eyes.

'You quarrelled?'

'No, I was upset and I just left.' He turned away to hide his tears. 'I went home.'

'What time was this?'

'I don't know. It wasn't dark.'

'You stayed at home?'

'No, I went back later; I couldn't settle. It was quite dark then; there was no light in the flat and I thought that Fran must have gone to bed . . . I couldn't bring myself to disturb her . . . I wish to God I had.'

'So what did you do?'

'I spent the night here – I do that sometimes. There's a sort of bed at the end there.' He pointed down the workshop.

'I noticed a spare bed in the bedroom upstairs; did you never spend the night there?'

'Never.'

'So last night you were here in the workshop.'

A nod. 'If I'd gone up to her when I arrived back here I might have . . . ' His voice choked on the words.

Wycliffe said, 'No, I don't think so.' After a brief pause he added, 'And when you went upstairs, early this morning, you found her.'

'Yes.' The word was barely audible.

Wycliffe tried again. 'Why did she move out of Mynhager to come here?'

Paul shook his head. 'It was her idea and it seemed the thing to do. I mean, we were working together here and I thought that we would end up by living together, but that was not what Fran wanted.'

'But you worked well together?'

'Oh, yes.' He pointed vaguely at the figures grouped together on the floor. 'All those figures are Fran's work, and they're good. I'm no use at working in the round.' He stopped speaking. It was clear that he wanted to say more but he had difficulty in making up his mind. In the end it came. In a low voice he said, 'I can't help wondering if all that has happened was because of the money.'

'What money?'

'Fran was left quite a lot of money by a relative. I don't know any details.'

'Didn't she speak to you about it?'

'No. I only got to hear of it from gossip on the site. They were saying that Fran wanted to buy herself into some sort of partnership with the Archers.'

'You didn't ask her about it?'

'No. If she wanted to discuss it with me she would have told me. So far as I was concerned it made no difference, but it was after she knew about the money that . . . Well, it was then that things changed.'

Wycliffe decided on a different line; the money angle could wait. 'Did you ever have the impression that Francine wanted to avoid a closer relationship because you were her half-brother?'

Perched on the edge of the bench Paul was staring down at his feet. He spoke quietly. 'She said that, but I knew it wasn't true. It was just an excuse. She didn't want me.' The words were spoken with bleak resignation.

A pause, then he looked up. 'But what does it matter now?'

Wycliffe decided that he must begin to act like a policeman. He said, 'I want you to go with one of my officers to Penzance Police Station where you will be asked to make a statement for the record.'

'Am I under arrest?'

Wycliffe took pity. 'No, Paul, and you are not accused of anything. This is routine, which follows inevitably from the fact that you were close to Francine and that you were here last night. You understand?'

'Yes.'

Wycliffe walked down the length of the workshop to an area at the back where wood was stored in racks. In a corner there was a camp bed with a mattress, a pillow of sorts and two or three blankets.

Outside, Lucy, who had sat through the whole interview but had not spoken a word, said, 'Do you want me to warn them of his arrival? They'll need to be briefed.'

'No. Kersey will be going to Penzance and Paul can travel with him. I would like him to conduct the interview and I'll have a word. Put him in the picture.'

Chapter Three

Whit-Sunday continued

Lucy pointed across the stream to a substantial two-storied house with a lichen-covered slate roof. 'That's where the Archers live, and the Guild office is there.'

The sun was shining, and the moor was a pattern of greens with splashes of yellow gorse, dotted with grey boulders and crag-like outcrops of granite.

They found the office at the side of the house. It was well-equipped and business-like but unattended. There was a bell on the desk which Lucy pressed, and in due time a wispy little woman, grey-haired and sixtyish, came through from the house. She wore an apron, and she was wiping her hands on a towel.

She looked at Wycliffe. 'Oh, I remember you. You're the policeman. I thought they might send you.'

Wycliffe was puzzled, then recognition dawned. Yet another figure from the past – Evadne Penrose; he remembered her name. Not bad after ten years. But she seemed to have shrivelled, as though sun-dried: her face was a network of wrinkles.

Pleased with himself, he said, 'You're Mrs Penrose. You were a friend of the Lemarques and you lived in Wesley Terrace.'

The little woman was unimpressed. 'Yes, I'm Evadne Penrose and I was a friend of Jane Lemarque but I couldn't say the same of her husband or, for that matter, of her daughter, though I wouldn't have had this happen to anybody. Yes, I still live in Wesley Terrace but I come here to help out.'

Wycliffe tried to stay clever. 'I remember that you were interested in astrology.'

'I'm not only interested, as you put it, I *believe* that our destiny is influenced by the celestial sphere, and during the last ten years I've been making a serious study of the subject. That's why I'm here. Archer and I have a lot in common – including the fact that we are both Sagittarians.' She added, 'But you didn't come here to talk to me.'

It took Wycliffe a moment to recover. 'I want to talk to everybody who has anything to tell me about Francine and her relationships.'

Pouted lips. 'Yes, well, Francine was a Scorpio.' She broke off. 'Anyway, I'll get them to talk to you.' And she was gone.

A moment or two later a large and distinguished-looking man came through from the house, already talking. 'My name is Archer – Francis Bacon Archer. This is a terrible thing. I can't begin to take it in. I mean, that the poor girl should be murdered is bad enough, but here, of all places!'

Wycliffe introduced himself and Lucy Lane.

'Do sit down, both of you.' A gracious manner.

He was impressive, and there was something familiar about him. Wycliffe wondered whether he was yet another haunting from the past, then he remembered. He had been reading a biography of Eric Gill, and here was a photofit of the man on the cover: the father of the twentieth-century craft colony.

The image came complete, with the beautifully sculptured silky hair, the beard and the moustache. Even the spectacles were right – narrow lenses with pale rims. No doubt there was a round, broad-brimmed, black hat somewhere handy, even if there was no stone-carver's smock in a closet.

Archer's choice of a role model said much about the man himself, but he had adopted astrology as his religion, instead of Gill's aberrant, if colourful, Roman Catholicism. Wycliffe wondered if he shared Gill's sexual proclivities. No doubt that would emerge.

And the expansive manner was there. 'We shall miss her greatly, both as a person and as a craftswoman. She and Paul Batemen were a well-matched pair: Francine's best work was done in the round, while Paul is a real master of relief.'

They sat down. Was it by chance that Archer's desk was placed so that the soft light from the window did justice to his profile?

Already mildly prejudiced, Wycliffe got down to business. 'I understand that Francine Lemarque had been a Guild member for some years and that for several weeks she occupied the flat above the wood-carvers' workshop where, last night, she was murdered.'

A pause, to let the brutal word sink in. Then, 'We need you to tell us what you can about her way of life and her relationships – anything which might shed light on her death.'

Archer stroked his beard. 'I am in a very difficult position, Mr Wycliffe. Francine came to us after serving a sentence in a Young Offenders' institution, and it was only because of her association with Paul Bateman, and the fact that she had taken a course in wood-carving while in custody, that, after a trial period, we felt able to offer her a place here.'

Archer sat back in his chair. 'She spent some months in my gallery in St Ives as a sort of probation. I— '

Wycliffe cut him short. 'I know her earlier history very well, Mr Archer. And I know that she was not directly related to the Bishop family at Mynhager. If any of this turns out to be relevant we already have material to work on. You can best help by telling us about her life here, particularly during recent months.'

Archer readjusted his ego. 'I'll try.'

Wycliffe went on, 'I've already spoken to Paul and he has gone to Penzance Police Station to make a statement as a witness to the circumstances.'

Archer clasped his hands on the desk top. 'We are very worried about Paul, Mr Wycliffe. Since Francine came to live with us on the site he has changed. I know nothing of the details but it has been obvious to anyone that things had not gone the way he had hoped and expected.'

'How did Francine fit in with the other members of your Guild?'

Archer shifted in his chair. 'I don't know whether you have any knowledge of astrology, Mr Wycliffe, but I have made some study of the subject. Francine was a Scorpio, born early in the month of November, and I have to say that she was in every way true to her birth sign. Scorpios are secretive and intense, with tremendous will-power. They are inclined to be ruthless and they can be dangerous enemies.'

'You are saying, then, that she did not fit in; perhaps that her presence here was disruptive?'

This was too direct for Archer and he side-stepped. 'We are craftsmen, Mr Wycliffe, and each of us is absorbed in the very individual work we have on hand, but I have to admit that we do not always achieve that sense of community and mutual trust for which I have hoped and worked.'

Wycliffe was losing patience. 'Whatever that may mean, Mr Archer, DS Lane will be spending some time here, with others, inquiring into Francine's relationships, and you and your members will, as a matter of routine, be required to account for those relationships as far as possible.'

Lucy Lane came in on cue. 'To start we shall need a list of the people who work here and the names of any regular visitors.'

Archer seemed about to protest. 'I assure you, Mr Wycliffe— '

It was at that moment Wycliffe became aware of a tallish blonde woman, standing in the doorway which led from the house. Archer must have seen her at the same moment and he became flustered. 'Oh, Lina, my dear! . . . Do join us . . . Superintendent Wycliffe and Sergeant Lane are here about poor Francine.'

Then, to Wycliffe, 'This is my wife and partner in our enterprise. She is a painter, but she now concerns herself more with the business side.'

Lina came into the room, closing the door behind her, and took the chair Archer placed for her. She wore a turtle-neck jumper with expensively tailored trousers. Well-packaged elegance.

Wycliffe had the impression that she had been waiting, ready prepared to make her entrance. Younger than Archer? Perhaps, but not much; there were tell-tale lines around her mouth and eyes.

As she sat down she took charge. 'It is obvious that Mr Wycliffe wants to know more of the nature of our Guild, of our work and of our relationships. In the circumstances that seems perfectly reasonable and we must help in any way we can.'

Knowing her background, Wycliffe was impressed by her remarkable command of English.

Archer said, 'My wife is Dutch; we met when she was working in the conservation department of the Rijksmuseum in Amsterdam.' From his manner it was evident that Archer still had pride in his Trojan horse.

Lina leaned forward in her chair, resting her hands lightly on the table top. 'Anything we can do to assist your inquiries we shall do gladly.'

Wycliffe said, 'Perhaps you will tell us something of the nature of your Guild and how it works.'

'Of course. Our conditions require that there shall be nine of us engaged in art and craft work which we market as a group. We find it convenient and pleasant to work and, in some cases, to live together as a community. Apart from Archer and myself, Paul and Francine, whom you already know about, we have a very distinguished potter in Derek Scawn. He lives on the site with his assistant, Robert Lander, who, I believe, is some sort of relative but he is not a member of the Guild.'

She broke off with a glance at Lucy, who was taking notes. 'Am I going too quickly for you?'

Lucy was reassuring and Lina continued. 'And there are three more – Emile Collis, our resident painter; Alice Field, who looks after miniature crafts and Arthur Gew, our typographer and engraver.'

A satisfied smile. 'And there, I think, you have us.'

Lucy Lane said, 'So, at the moment, you seem to be one member short.'

Lina shifted in her chair. 'You are quick, Miss Lane. Yes, we do have a vacancy at present. Some months ago the young woman who ran our jewellery department left us. The department was not a success and there is some discussion about how she should be replaced. Derek Scawn has nominated his assistant, Robert Lander, for the vacancy but at the moment it remains open.'

Lina, satisfied that she had dealt successfully with a minor hiccup could not resist embroidering. She went on. 'Of course, in any group such as ours there are bound to be currents and cross-currents, but in a terrible situation like this they are easily exaggerated.

'Anyway, to complete our story, I should add that, as a quite separate business, Archer has his own gallery in St Ives where he sells paintings and craft work.'

She sat back, pleased with herself. 'I'm quite sure that Archer will have no objection to you meeting and talking to any or all of us if it will help. In fact, you had better have one of our brochures. At least it will identify the people I have mentioned.' She reached into a drawer. 'And here are some copies of our site plan which will help you to find them.'

A polished performance which left no doubt about who was running the show, and Wycliffe found himself mildly bewildered, with a fistful of glossy art work.

He gathered the reins and his wits. 'Thank you. That was very clear. Now, perhaps, we can concentrate on Francine and her relationships with the others. For example, Mr Archer mentioned that in recent weeks there appears to have been some tension between Francine and Paul Bateman.'

A pursing of lips. Lina said, 'There is, I believe, a simple explanation for that. Francine was spending too much time with Emile Collis, our painter.'

'You think there was something between them?'

A dismissive gesture. 'I think Francine was merely being provocative.'

'Another point: I understand that Francine had come into money and that there was some question of her investing in the Guild. Could this have been a source of friction?'

Lina was ready. 'I wondered when we would come to that. And I have to say that indirectly it could have given rise to tension. Francine told me that she had inherited a substantial sum from an aunt and that she would be interested in a possible investment in the Guild.'

'You were willing to consider such a proposal?'

Lina glanced at her husband. 'To consider it – yes. But there were difficulties in that it would have entailed substantial changes in the nature and organisation of the Guild.'

'Were these possible changes resented by the others?'

Lina looked mildly uncomfortable. 'I suppose you could say that there was resentment in some quarters.'

'Presumably you had discussions with her?'

'I went to see her one evening with a view to finding out exactly what her position was, and to explain ours. Of course, there was no question of reaching any decisions at that stage. We simply had a discussion that was entirely amicable.'

'When was this?'

'I talked to Francine on Friday evening.'

'You visited her in her flat?'

'Yes.'

'At what time did you leave?'

'I can't say exactly. It was dusk.' A sharp look. 'Is this important?'

Wycliffe did not answer directly. 'We believe that Francine died in the late evening or early in the night on Saturday, the day following your visit, but the obstruction could have been put in place at any time before that. It would become effective only when she used the bath heater. The vent is visible from several places on the site and though the obstruction itself might not be noticed, anyone putting it there in daylight would be conspicuous.'

'So someone may have put whatever it was there during darkness on Friday night. Are you suggesting— ?'

'Certainly not. I am simply inquiring into the possibility that someone may have been seen on the balcony or in the vicinity. Every possibility, however unlikely, has to be followed up.'

'All I can say is that I saw no one.' Lina was flustered.

Wycliffe decided that it was a good point at which to break off.

He stood up. 'Well, thank you for your help. DS Lane will be here with others to talk to the rest of the Guild members and it will be necessary later to take formal statements in some cases. Being Sunday, I suppose there will be few people on the site?'

Lina was dismissive. 'We don't work to fixed hours or days, Mr Wycliffe. It depends on what commissions we have. And, of course, some of us live here anyway. As a matter of fact, I think we prefer having our free time when the shops are open, so it is quite possible that we may have a full house today.' Lina evidently took pride in her mastery of colloquial English.

Wycliffe had had as much as he could take in one session, but on the point of leaving, he said, 'I see you have Evadne Penrose working for you.'

Archer looked surprised. 'You know her? . . . Of course, she was a friend of Jane Lemarque and you would have met her then.'

Lina cut in. 'I hardly think Evadne would agree that she works for us – rather that she helps us out. You may not know that she is a firm believer in astrology. And, like Archer, she is a Sagittarian, so what more could we ask?'

They were seen off by Archer, and outside Wycliffe said, 'So there we are! The best butter, nicely wrapped. Now it's over to you, Lucy. I'm not asking you to do a hut-to-hut. Just pick out one or two you think might be interesting and go fishing. Obviously we shall have to interview them all formally when we've more to go on.'

'May I ask, sir, what you intend to do?'

'I'm hoping to renew an acquaintance of ten years ago; a chap called Marsden, a painter. If he's still around and on form he'll know a good deal of what goes on here. Whether he'll tell me about it is another matter, but there's no harm in trying.'

'And where does this oracle live?'

'I'll show you. I want you to drive me there before you start here. By the way, what's the time?'

'If you look at the clock on the dash you'll see that it says three forty-five.' Lucy was nobody's nanny.

'What about trying for a snack at the Tributers'?'

'One of your better ideas, sir, if you think they'll bother with us at this time of the day.'

'I've got friends around here, Lucy. At least I hope I have.'

The Tributers' was empty except for a plump woman behind the bar polishing glasses. She looked up, hesitated, then, 'Mr Wycliffe! My dear life! It must be ten year if it's a day!'

Phyllis Tregigo at sixty, still looking as plump and rosy-cheeked as ever on a diet which figured eggs, bacon, pasties and cream high on the menu.

'Good to see you again, Phyllis. This is Detective Sergeant Lane.'

'Pleased to meet you, my dear. And there was me thinking he'd brought his wife to see me like he promised all they years back.' She turned to Wycliffe, 'Ah, well! I suppose you're mixed up with this business on the moor. I thought you must've got too high up for that sort of thing but I'm some glad you're here.'

'We wondered if you could manage a sandwich or two and a cup of coffee?'

Later, leaving The Tributers' after a salad with home-cured ham, Lucy said, 'I must add Phyllis Tregigo to my list of your fans.'

They turned off the coast road down a narrow lane by the pub. A little blue and white sign read, 'To Mulfra Headland and Cove'. Two or three cottages and the lane became a dirt track with a low granite wall against rising ground to the right, and the steep sides of a barren valley to the left. Down there the same stream which flowed through the craft site made its tortuous way to the sea.

Across the valley a single cottage stood in isolation. The Lemarques had lived there: Francine, with her mother and the man she believed to be her father. More memories. It was ten years ago but nothing seemed to have changed. As if to drive home the point it started to rain. Then it was Christmas; now it was spring.

They came to Marsden's cottage: the lean-to studio was still there and its glass roof still had its quota of gull droppings, essential, according to Marsden, for filtering the light.

Lucy pulled up by the cottage. 'You'd better check that he's in before I leave you.'

'He's in all right; can't you hear?' Music was blasting out of the cottage and Wycliffe recognised a Verdi chorus, though with Marsden it might equally have been Gregorian chant or the Spice Girls. A man of catholic tastes.

'Come back in about an hour, Lucy. I've got my mobile if you want to get in touch before then.'

Lucy found a place to reverse and drove off.

Wycliffe banged on the door and eventually the music died, the door opened and there was Marsden filling the gap. 'My God, it's the Law!' Marsden would have made a good drinking partner for Sir Toby Belch, up to all his tricks. He hadn't changed much: his face was a little fatter, his colour a trifle higher and his dark curls had given way to a grey fuzz.

'Do come in! How long is it? Must be seven or eight years.'

'It's more like ten.'

The room hadn't changed much either. It was spartan, with coir matting on the stone floor, a cupboard, a kitchen table and chairs, and a couple of Windsors by an open grate where damp logs smouldered.

Add a state-of-the-art music centre, a storage cabinet for records and CDs. What was both new and surprising was a telephone.

A cat sprawled, paws extended, by the hearth.

'Is that still Percy?'

'Of course it's Percy. We wear well in this neck of the woods, don't we, boy?' And he nudged the cat gently with the toe of his slipper. 'Can you do with a beer? Tributers' home brew. Remember?'

Once settled, Wycliffe said, 'Francine Lemarque – I suppose you've heard?'

'Nobody tells me anything. What about Fran?'

'She was found dead in her bed this morning.' Wycliffe described the circumstances.

Marsden was silent for a while, then he said, 'Poor little Fran! That kid never had any luck . . . You've got the bastard who did it?'

'No.' Wycliffe told what he knew.

'You're not saying you think it was the boy? Paul couldn't kill a louse. And he was daft about her. You must remember how he danced to her tune when they were schoolkids. And when your lot got her put away he never missed a visit. Nothing's changed.'

'Did she ever come to see you?'

'Now and then, when she was feeling browned-off.'

'When was she last here?'

Marsden frowned. 'About a week ago.'

'What did you talk about?'

'Anything or nothing.'

'But you must have known that she'd left Mynhager and was living in a flat above their workshop in the Archer set-up. The fact is, I'd like to know more about this Guild of Nine.'

Marsden paused with the tankard to his lips. 'I'm getting the message. You've heard on the grapevine that Marsden sometimes puts in an appearance there, so if there's any dirt he'll know about it even if he isn't up to his neck in it.'

He looked at Wycliffe. 'Is that how it goes?'

'Not quite, but it will do.'

Marsden took time to consider and finally he said, 'Our Lina is the brains behind that outfit.'

'Lina being Archer's wife?'

'The boy is quick. Anyway, I don't know of anything crooked going on there. She runs a good business. They've sold some of my stuff and got fair prices. True, they take a nice whack for the kitty but I'm not whingeing on that account.'

'So a thriving business, well run and above board. I'm glad to hear it.'

Marsden spoke into his beer. 'Like hell you are. You smell a rat or you wouldn't be here.'

Wycliffe said nothing and after a while Marsden went on, 'Lina is away quite a bit.'

'So?'

'For one thing she makes regular visits back home; I'd say five or six times a year. You know she's Dutch?'

Wycliffe said, 'I'm told that Archer met her when she worked in the Rijksmuseum in Amsterdam.'

Marsden made a dismissive gesture. 'Archer is a stuffed dummy, but Lina manages for both of 'em. Anyway, on these visits back home she attends picture auctions.'

'Does she buy much?'

'There must be one or two auctioneers in the business who are not sorry to see her among the punters. She's known.'

'What does she buy?'

Marsden jibbed at these direct questions. 'How should I know? I only pick up a bit here and there from old mates when they're this way, or if they phone, needing a spot of local colour quick.'

In the ensuing silence Percy drew himself together, standing on all fours, arching his back and stretching. Then he mewed plaintively at Marsden.

Marsden said, 'Percy wants to go out. Bladder's getting weaker, like mine.'

When Marsden returned he sat for a while, supping his beer and staring into the fire. Wycliffe knew better than to try to hurry him.

And in the end it came. 'There's something odd about the way she spreads her money. I mean, she doesn't stick to a period or a group or a style. The subject doesn't seem to matter much either. As long as it's by a name, with a reasonable provenance and within her price range, that's all she seems to care about.'

'And what is her range?'

'Anything from five to ten grand. She never gets carried away and tops that. Don't ask me what ten grand is in guilders or euros but it's real money anywhere, though she's not playing against the big boys.'

'You've been keeping an eye on her.'

Marsden shifted heavily in his chair. 'I admit that along with one or two mates who travel, we've got interested. We're intrigued because we can't see what she's up to.'

'Do you know what happens to the pictures?'

'She sells them on, of course. She's not setting up a bloody gallery. With the few I've been able to trace, she's made a bit. But on balance, after allowing for expenses and commission, it's doubtful if she does more than break even. The game doesn't seem worth the candle. It's odd. That's all.'

'A hobby?'

Marsden sighed and scratched his forehead. 'Perhaps. I suppose Shylock could have had a hobby, but I wouldn't bet on it.'

Wycliffe thought it time to try a fresh move. 'Do you know Emile Collis?'

'Lina's poodle. Is she trying to involve him?'

'I did get that impression. Why? Is Francine really supposed to have had designs on this man?'

Marsden shrugged. 'If Fran showed any interest in Collis it wasn't for what he had to offer in bed. Even with Lina you can bet that it would be a matter of property rather than petting.'

'How does he rank as a painter?'

'He's a first-rate draughtsman and a good technician – knows his colours and how to handle them, but he's short on imagination. Anyway, he's known for the sort of thing he does, and he sells.'

'I suppose most of the Guild output is marketed through Archer's gallery in St Ives?'

Marsden laughed. 'Then you suppose wrong. No way! Most of it is sold in London – Lina again. The paintings go to Oldberg in Mason's Yard, or to the Raphael in Grafton Street. For the craft work she gets specific commissions from the London stores and from abroad; mainly from the States.'

'So where does Archer come in?'

Marsden grinned. 'He paints pretty little pictures which he peddles in his gallery along with Guild stuff which isn't quite up to the London market. Generally, he's no more than a sort of animated extension of their logo. A good front.'

A pause before he added, 'Sometimes I feel sorry for the poor bugger.'

Wycliffe tried again. 'When Fran came here did she ever mention Lina's Amsterdam pictures?'

Marsden frowned. 'Yes, she did, and it surprised me that she knew about them. She was interested and tried to pump me as you have, but there was nothing I could tell her more than I've told you.'

'Did she tell you that she'd come into money?'

'No. Had she?'

'From the Bristol aunt who came down when she was in trouble before.'

Marsden sighed. 'Poor Fran. Just her luck. Now I suppose some other bugger will get the fun of it.'

Wycliffe stood up. He had what he came for: the recovery of times past along with a useful background to the Archer enterprise, but something remained and he approached the subject, unsure of Marsden's response.

As though on a sudden thought, he asked, 'What happened to your portrait of Francine?'

'It's still where you saw it. I'm not parting with that. Not now, anyway. Want to take another look?'

Wycliffe followed him into the lean-to studio. The picture had acquired a new position, against one of the walls, and Marsden had gone to the expense of gallery-type lighting. The picture was covered with a drape which he removed.

And there it was again, a study in blues and greys and greens and purples, with a flush of pink in the flesh tones. A sixteen-year-old girl in a flowered wrap with one breast exposed. She was watching herself in a mirror.

Wycliffe remembered Marsden's words: 'She's catching a glimpse of the promised land and not sure that she's going to like it . . . She's on the threshold . . . Another week, another month, she'll have crossed over. And nobody will ever see that look again . . . But I've captured it on canvas . . . Like a butterfly pinned in a box . . . '

It was true, and Wycliffe felt humbled. It distressed him to think that a couple of hours ago he had seen what had happened to this young girl after she had crossed that threshold.

Marsden was still looking at his painting and suddenly, unexpectedly, he chuckled. 'After sitting for me for two or three

51

hours with breaks, looking like that, she would slip off the throne, pull up her dress to cover herself and say, "That's eight quid you owe me." '

He sighed. 'There'll never be another Francine.' And he added, 'At the right time I intended to give her that picture. Occasionally, on one of her visits, she would come in here, switch on the lights and stand in front of it, but she never made any comment – not a word.'

Wycliffe felt guilty. 'I must admit that I lost sight of her after the trial.'

'You couldn't have exerted yourself; she was easy enough to find. Bloody coppers! You're all the same underneath. She was paroled after three years. She should never have been sentenced.'

'She killed a man.'

'She stepped on a cockroach.'

It was strange. Ever since he had arrived on the moor that morning Wycliffe had had the feeling that he was taking up where he'd left off; picking up the threads. And it was not pleasant.

The truth was that he had tried hard to forget. There had never been a case in which he had become so personally, even emotionally, entangled, and now he was faced with a tragic sequel.

Marsden saw him off. 'Copper or no, there are worse about, so if you're going to be around for a day or two, you know where I live.'

Wycliffe stood outside the cottage, wondering about his next move. No sign of Lucy yet. He turned to Marsden. 'If my sergeant comes knocking on the door tell her I've gone on to Mynhager.'

'You'll see changes there.'

'Do you still see anything of Caroline?'

Marsden grinned. 'Now and then. Like when Easter Monday falls on a Tuesday. Then we celebrate for old time's sake. What's it got to do with you, anyway?'

It had stopped raining and there was a watery sun. He walked on a couple of hundred yards around the next bend, and there was the sea and the cove and the cliffs, and that crazy house.

It was there that he had spent that Christmas. It was there

that the Bishop family had lived and still lived. And it was there that Francine Lemarque had shot her father, Gerald Bateman MP, a rising politician, a minister-in-waiting and a murderer twice over.

Wycliffe told himself, I've got to face it sometime, so it might as well be now.

'Alice Field, Craftwork in Miniature'. According to the plan this mysterious activity was carried on in a little building close to the entrance and Lucy decided to start there. Through the window she could see a young blonde woman bending over a low bench doing something to the roof of a dolls' house.

Her reception was friendly. 'Are you from the police? . . . I'm trying to work but it's impossible to settle down to anything. I mean . . . It's scarcely believable.'

'Detective Sergeant Lane – Lucy.' It was not difficult to see that informality was the recipe for the day.

'I'm Alice – Alice Field. You've probably been briefed by our Lina.'

Lucy looked about her and marvelled at the variety and perfection of the little models.

Alice said, 'Yes, it's an odd way to earn a living.'

'Not as odd as mine sometimes.'

'So, about poor Fran— '

'You knew her, of course.'

'Find yourself a stool.' Then, 'Yes, I knew her. In a way she was a friend and it's hard to realise that she's gone. She came here whenever she was bored with her own work or at cross-purposes with Paul . . . God knows how he'll cope without her . . . Yes, I suppose I knew her as well as most.'

'Then you can help us. We are trying to piece together what we can about her and her relationships here and outside. I understand that there had been strains between her and Paul since she came to live in the flat.'

'You've been listening to our Lina but I suppose there's something in what she says.'

'In particular she hinted that it might have something to do with Francine's relationship with the painter, Emile Collis.'

After a longish pause Alice said, 'I know that she and Emile were spending time together. Emile was doing a series of sketches in preparation for a portrait which I think he had begun to paint. He sees himself as a frustrated portrait painter, and with a model like Fran what more could he have wanted? Fran told me about it herself.'

She summed up. 'I think it's very unlikely that there was sex involved.'

'Lina made it pretty clear that she thought Francine was leading him up the garden and making him miserable. Would you say that she was a tease with men?'

Alice considered. 'Don't forget I work here. But I will say this, I'm sure that for some weeks Emile has been a very worried man but I doubt if his worries have had much to do with Francine.'

'Have you any idea what is worrying him?'

'Not a clue. I know him as somebody who's always around and that's about all. He has very little to say for himself but he seems well in with the Archers.'

'Lina mentioned another man – apparently he works in the pottery— '

Alice grinned. 'Bob Lander – Blond Bob, as they call him. Somehow I don't think Fran would have got far with him. He seems a nice enough sort of bloke but my guess is that women don't interest him – not as such, anyway.' She broke off, 'Talk of the devil— '

Through the window Lucy had a glimpse of a sturdy, muscular young man, on the short side, with almost yellow hair. He wore a leather jacket and he was leaving the site on foot.

Alice said, 'My guess is that he and Emile could have something going for them, but don't quote me.' A brief pause, then, 'By the way, could you do with a coffee?'

'I thought you'd never ask.'

A few minutes later, when they were drinking their mugs of instant, Lucy asked, 'Do you live on the site?'

'Good Lord, no! I've got a house and a husband in St Ives. There are three of us who don't live here, although sometimes we might as well.'

'It would help if you could tell me something of the set-up, and perhaps where Francine fitted in – or didn't. This Guild of Nine – what exactly is it?'

Alice smiled. 'I expect you've already had Lina's version.'

'I would like yours. I understand that there are supposed to be nine of you.'

'Yes. Archer has a thing about numbers and there has to be nine of us, the mystical trinity of trinities and all that stuff. Added to that, there's his name, and the fact that he was born under the sign of Sagittarius, the Archer, in the ninth house of the Zodiac. There you have it all as I understand it, including our logo.'

She smiled. 'Archer is quite likeable in many ways but he plays at life like a child. He wanted to start a craft colony resurrecting Eric Gill's at Pigotts, but this isn't the thirties and he's certainly no Eric Gill.' She laughed. 'Neither as a craftsman nor as a womaniser.

'Anyway Lina let him go ahead, but she turned his dream colony into a small-scale factory that makes a respectable profit.'

All grist to the mill.

A moment later Alice said, 'Going back to Francine and being honest, she made something of a reputation for being a bit of a tease with men. All go to a certain point then, "You're in the wrong shop, Buster!"' A moment of hesitation. 'I don't think it was like that. Not so long ago she talked to me about her attitude to sex.'

'And?'

'I sometimes had the impression that sex scared her. She might even have felt guilty because of it. Of course she put up a show along the lines of not being at the beck and call of any man. The emancipated woman and all that, but I sometimes wondered how deep it really went.'

Alice brushed back her hair from her eyes. 'One thing's for sure, Paul suffered, poor man. He doted on her and got precious little in return.'

Lucy finished her coffee. 'You've been a great help. You wouldn't believe how difficult it is, breaking into other people's lives, and that's what much of this job amounts to.'

Alice nodded. 'I think I'll stick to making toys for well-heeled types who want to relive their childhood.'

Chapter Four

Whit-Sunday evening continued

The bells of Mulfra church were ringing, the light was golden and there was a great stillness. Once more Wycliffe found himself standing in the stone-walled courtyard in front of the Gothic door studded with nails. Nothing had changed. Even their old Rover was still parked on the cobbles. It looked like a hearse and was well on the way to being a museum piece, yet Wycliffe still felt he had gone back all of those ten years to that Christmas visit.

He tugged at the wrought-iron chain and heard the bell clang. At last the door opened and there, as on that first visit, was Caroline, looking a little older, a little fatter, her mouth a little slacker.

'Charles!' She opened the door wide. 'You can't believe how relieved I am to see you . . . We thought we might be dealing with some stranger . . . *Do* come in.'

Of all the possible receptions he might have anticipated this was the most bizarre. Caroline was close to offering her cheek to be kissed. Yet his last visit had ended in a manslaughter and a murder charge, both affecting the family.

He was taken into the drawing room which seemed poised over the cove, its essential tattiness drowned in a great flood of light from the sea.

Virginia arrived; her welcome was more restrained but she did not disguise her relief. 'Now we shall get some sense!'

A trousered Virginia, a little leaner, a little bonier and a voice that had acquired a masculine resonance.

Caroline said, 'Paul has gone out walking, poor lad. On his own, of course. There's nothing anybody can do or say to help him. This, on top of all that's gone before. I only hope to God that he doesn't do anything foolish—' She broke off and turned sharply to Wycliffe, struck by a new and frightening possibility. '*You* don't suspect him of . . . of what happened to Fran, do you?'

Wycliffe hesitated, then decided that there are times when it is right to stop being a policeman and try being human. 'No, I don't. I think I know Paul well enough to understand that he is incapable of such a coldly premeditated crime.'

Caroline let out a deep sigh and turned to her sister. 'There! I told you we would be safe if only it could be Charles who came.'

Wycliffe decided it was time to assume control. 'I want to ask you about Francine. I understand that she chose to come here when she was released on parole and that she lived here until quite recently.'

It was Virginia who responded. 'Yes, it was an extraordinary situation but we felt that we must do what we could. Father, Aunt Stella and Ernest, our brother, had all passed away during those three years, so we had only ourselves to consider. Paul, of course, wanted it above all else. Although still a teenager he had visited her regularly while she was in the Young Offenders, and it was only through his persistence that we eventually succeeded in getting her on the craft course in wood-carving.'

'So what happened when she came here?'

Virginia sighed. 'It's a long story. Paul was already one of Archer's precious Guild of Nine as a wood-carver, and eventually Fran joined him, first as an assistant, and later, when there was a vacancy in the Guild, as a member herself. They made a good team apparently and until recently it seemed that things were beginning to go their way.'

Virginia was sitting in one of the easy chairs, legs crossed. She lit a cigarette and watched the smoke spiral upwards.

'So what changed?'

It was Caroline's turn. 'It happened from one day to the next. Out of the blue, it seemed, Francine decided to move out of here and she went to live in the flat over their workshop.'

'What was Paul's reaction?'

Virginia again. 'You will remember that at sixteen Paul was infatuated with Fran, though I admit she gave him little encouragement. That situation never really changed, even when the poor lad discovered that his adored girlfriend was his half-sister. He visited her whenever he could while she was in custody and when she came out they seemed to take up where they left off; but living here and working together. It seemed that they had accepted their ambivalent relationship.'

Wycliffe realised that he might be treading on thin ice, and he chose his words with care. 'Do you think that Francine moved to the flat in order to have greater freedom in her relationship with Paul?'

Caroline said, 'You mean so that they could go to bed together without upsetting me. That's what Vee thinks.'

Virginia hesitated. 'I'm not sure that I do.'

Caroline snapped, 'You said it was sex.'

Virginia reached out to tap ash from her cigarette into a monstrous Canton jar. 'I say a lot of things but I don't believe this move had anything to do with Paul. I think he was puzzled by it.'

Caroline said, 'You see! Although I'm his mother he talks to her.'

And Virginia came back. 'That's because you never listen!'

Wycliffe felt he could get no further. What good would it do to mention the money? Paul would tell them at some stage. Sufficient unto the day . . . He left, promising to keep in touch.

Lucy, deciding that discretion might be the better part, had parked some way up the track and he joined her. It was Lucy's first sight of Mynhager.

'It's fantastic! It's like a backdrop for the Rhine Maidens.'

They swapped stories and Lucy said, 'Do we tackle Collis before going back?'

'No. He and the rest can wait until we're organised. We'll get back to Penzance and see what we've got in the way of an Incident Room.'

They set out for Penzance. Sunday evening, and they had the moorland road to themselves. Even when they reached the town many of the streets were deserted.

They were booked in at an hotel on the Promenade. The same hotel in which Wycliffe had stayed years before, during investigations into the murder of a Penzance bookseller. They joined Kersey for the evening meal.

'What did you make of Paul Bateman?'

Kersey stroked his bristly chin. 'Good question, and the answer is that I wouldn't expect him to kill a garden slug. But he was obsessed by that girl and, I guess, profoundly frustrated.' Kersey paused before adding, 'He certainly had opportunity, but motive? . . . It's hard to say exactly what the word means in this context.'

Kersey launching into semantics was a surprising phenomenon, but Wycliffe saw his point.

'On balance?'

'I don't think he'd top my list if I had one. Anyway, he made his statement and I sent him back home in a patrol car.'

'Back home?'

'To his mother at Mynhager. That's where he said he wanted to go.'

Later, Wycliffe stood at his bedroom window looking out over the bay, with the Lizard light sweeping the sky to the south-east, and the magic Mount, Island of Ictis, a twinkling silhouette in the foreground. He felt that he wanted to praise somebody for something but he wasn't quite sure who, or for what.

He telephoned Helen instead.

End of an eventful day, Whit Sunday.

That night Wycliffe dreamed that he was alone in Marsden's studio. Greatly daring, he removed the drape from the portrait of Francine. It was as he remembered it. Except for the face . . . The face was that of the girl on the bed, corrupted by the ravages of death.

He awoke, distressed and fearful, like a child after a bad dream.

He had a restless night and by seven in the morning he was showered and dressed, waiting for the day to begin.

Whit Monday

Breakfast with Kersey and Lucy. News of the murder had spread and they were aware of attention from the sprinkling of tourists in the dining room. Kersey had the *Morning News* and he pointed to a brief front-page report, but the media had not yet grasped the colourful possibilities of the case.

As they walked to the police station a moist breeze was blowing off the sea. Whit Monday looked like being a day of sunshine and stealthy showers. For Wycliffe as a young boy Whit Monday had meant a picnic if the weather was fine, and the fair in the evening. But home by nine because father had milking in the morning.

The Incident Room was housed in one of those ubiquitous huts which clutter the breathing space behind most public buildings. As a plus, the place already had the regular nick smell, so everybody would feel at home. Already the organisation and equipment were well under way. By ten o'clock the team was assembled for Kersey's briefing. Remnants of the old guard included DCs Dixon and Potter – known because of Dixon's lean length and Potter's girth as Pole and Pot. Then there was the studious DC Curnow, a unique specimen – almost two metres of Penzance Cornishman. Curnow was reputed to spend his spare time reading and re-reading the *Encyclopaedia Britannica* from A to Z.

Added to these were the comparative newcomers, both of them women: the one and only DS Lucy Lane, now well on in her thirties, and DC Iris Thorne, the vivacious, no-nonsense black girl, who sometimes said, with notable effect, what others dared only to think.

Wycliffe, growing sentimental in his old age, looked them over with something very like affection.

The headquarters team was supplemented for the briefing by local CID and uniformed personnel who were, or were likely to become, involved.

Kersey explained the agreed programme which centred around systematic formal interviews with all those working or having regular business at the Guild site. It was arranged to have a caravan on the site that would be a temporary base for the team; the order and timing of such interviews to be arranged in consultation with DS Lane.

As Wycliffe put it to Kersey: 'We want first bite.'

Key witnesses would be required to make their statements for the record.

Questions were asked and answered. Wycliffe closed the proceedings with the obligatory blessing and the party broke up.

With Kersey and Lucy Lane, Wycliffe adjourned to the little room which had been set aside for him.

DS Fox arrived with his report.

Fox was a phenomenon; nobody really knew him. There was a nebulous wife. Children? It would probably be in his dossier but who reads dossiers? In any case they were flawed in that they trimmed gossip down to fact.

Fox's reports were models of their kind, and their preparation must have involved hours of his own time, yet the mere mention of his name was good for a smirk.

Now he laid his offerings on Wycliffe's table as though upon an altar. 'My report, sir; and the relevant documentation.' A neat bundle of typescript and a folder.

Wycliffe's defences went up. 'I'll need to go through all this but can you put us in the picture generally?'

Fox looked resigned; he was used to it. 'There are several items in my report, sir.'

'I'm sure there are, but— '

Fox stroked his long chin. 'I suppose there is only one really significant point: three months ago Francine Lemarque received a substantial legacy from an aunt.'

'We know there was a legacy, do you have any details – the amount, for example?'

'All the correspondence is there, sir.' Fox pointed to his file. 'The amount was something over eighty-five thousand pounds. It was left to her by an aunt.'

Kersey said, 'I wish I had a rich aunt.'

Wycliffe wondered about this aunt. Another figure emerging from the past? He recalled a brisk, kindly woman, clearly affluent, Francine's aunt on her mother's side but from a totally different milieu. Ten years ago she had turned up to comfort and care for Francine at crisis time – only to be rejected. Francine had no use for a shoulder to cry on.

'Was this aunt called Devlin?'

'I think that was the name, sir.'

Wycliffe, still reflective, said, 'So she's dead.'

'It would seem so, sir.'

Wycliffe sometimes suspected that these Jeevish responses were Fox's way of taking the mickey. And who could blame him for that? Wycliffe had long since decided that Fox was an enigma and, as that was one of his favourite words, it made him think more kindly of the man.

When Fox had gone, Kersey said, 'I wonder who gets the money?'

'Good question. But as a motive?' Wycliffe shook his head. 'There's much more to this case than money but we had better get Shaw down to look into that side of it.'

DS Shaw, born under the sign of the silicon chip, had somehow taken a wrong turning and found himself a policeman. Now he was the squad's front man in dealing with money and the disciples of money.

'At the same time he can go into the economics of the Guild and the fringe activities, whatever they are.'

Wycliffe was trying to get some sort of order into his own thoughts and at the same time to establish firm lines of inquiry. Along with much else he needed to check the records of possible suspects, likely and unlikely.

He skimmed through Fox's report and sifted through the remaining contents of the folder. Like most surviving remnants of a life they made a sad package: her pass book, four or five Christmas cards (one from Paul and another from the now deceased aunt), a little wad of business letters, some newspaper cuttings and, finally, two dog-eared engagement books, one for the current, and the other for the previous year. Wycliffe flicked through the pages of the current book and noticed that certain entries were inconspicuously starred. He checked, and found that the same was true of some of the later entries in the previous book. He passed them to Kersey. 'Get Iris to take a look at the starred entries and see what she makes of them.'

He glanced through the letters: six of them, clipped together, were from a firm of Bristol solicitors concerned with her legacy. He noticed that the first was addressed to her at Mynhager but the others were directed c/o The Guild of Nine. The dates made it clear that she had changed the address well before moving into the flat.

So the Bishops were to be kept in the dark about her legacy.

He turned to the newspaper cuttings. Francine hadn't seemed to him the sort to cut bits out of newspapers and he was interested. All the cuttings were from the local paper and concerned the Guild of Nine, chatty little pieces, evidently inspired by Lina.

One recent item referred to a possible extension of the Guild's activities into ornamental ironwork. Another was one of a series: 'Our Reporter Visits. This week, the Guild of Nine.'

Wycliffe had seen enough to be going on with. 'We'd better get moving, Lucy.'

They drove to Mulfra and on the way Wycliffe brooded, finally coming up with: 'I can't see this as a man's crime, Lucy.'

'You think that blocking up a flue outlet with a towel is more a woman's trick. Is that it?'

'It doesn't strike you that way?'

Lucy was driving, and she continued to look straight ahead. 'Devious and underhand; not like a good, honest, straightforward strangling or battering that we've come to expect from a man.'

Wycliffe grinned. 'All right, we won't halve the suspect list just yet.'

But Lucy had more to say. 'All the same, although I don't see it in a gender context, I think it might tell us something about the sort of person we are looking for.'

When they arrived the site displayed no unusual activity. In fact, none at all. They found two white-coated females from Forensic packing up in Francine's flat. Their report was unlikely to add much to what was already known, but hope springs eternal.

The senior of the two, Florence ('Please don't call me Flo'), was plump and didactic. 'Evidence from fingerprints suggests that the girl had three more or less regular male visitors and that one of them came much more frequently than the others, but there is nothing to indicate that he ever spent the night in the flat. There is a fairly fresh but smeared set of his prints on the bedroom doorpost. The indications are that he stood in the doorway for some time, supporting himself.'

Paul Bateman; and the other two would almost certainly have been Collis and the as yet unseen Blond Bob. Routine checks would settle these identities.

'Anything else?'

'There are two used sherry glasses which have remained by the sink for some time, unwashed. Both carry the prints of the dead girl but one has been used by another female. The implication being that there was a woman visitor at least a day before the crime.'

'Anything on the towel that blocked the vent?'

'An ordinary medium quality bath towel; no distinguishing marks but in the unlikely event that it had been used *and* that the user had left identifiable traces, I'm sending it for laboratory examination.'

Basic file fodder.

As at the start of any investigation Wycliffe began his search for the first hint of a pattern, but so far there was nothing. He was handicapped – or thought he was – by his inability to retain facts, to arrange them in an orderly fashion, and from them to arrive at logical conclusions. His mind didn't work that way. Any thread of logical thought soon became tangled in a web of recollected scenes, incidents, remarks and impressions.

He must hold on to the facts: Francine Lemarque had been murdered in a coldly calculating fashion. Some months earlier she had inherited a very substantial sum of money and, shortly after that, she had moved into the flat over the wood-carver's shop where she worked with her half-brother Paul Bateman.

Her treatment of Paul and her relations with Collis and Bob Lander had caused comment and, perhaps, jealousy. But that was a slender scaffolding on which to start building a case.

'We need to get more people talking, Lucy. More gossip.'

They were standing on the little balcony and Wycliffe was looking towards the neighbouring premises. 'The bigger building to the right is the pottery – the Scawn empire, if I remember rightly. What about the little place to our left?'

Lucy consulted her plan. 'Arthur Gew, typographer and engraver.'

'Right! You talk to Arthur. I'm going to take a stroll around to see the sights; then I might try my luck with Scawn and his side-kick, Lander.'

'We shall get some fresh points of view, if nothing else, and we can do with them.'

Arthur Gew. For some reason the name brought to Lucy's mind the image of a fussy, precise and reclusive little man, wielding his stylus or whatever, and wearing watchmaker's spectacles.

She was not far wrong. He was little, and he wore spectacles. He occupied a tiny room cluttered with apparatus and equipment of every description.

He was working with a stylus on a copper plate but he broke off and started talking at once. 'Whatever they've told you, I'm the Guild's dogsbody. Anything nobody else wants to do ends up here: wood- and copper-engraving, lettering, illumination, even the odd spot of enamelling – you name it.

'At the moment I'm designing personalised Christmas cards for a London barrister.'

He studied her, grey eyes peering over half-glasses. 'And you're a detective. You don't look like one but Madam told me on the phone that you were, so you must be. Madam is never wrong.'

Lucy got a word in. 'DS Lane. I'm making some general inquiries in connection with the death of Francine Lemarque.'

'Yes.' Reflective. 'Poor little bitch.'

'Is that how you saw her?'

'As a little bitch? More or less. She went around putting people's backs up as though it was her mission in life. She used to come here, poking and quizzing into everything, asking questions. And Madam let her get away with it. I don't know why – unless there was money involved. I've heard rumours.'

Lucy tried to direct the flow. 'You live over your workshop?'

'Yes. And I live alone. I don't get visitors and I'm neither homo nor hetero. I think that they must have neutered me at birth, and I'm grateful.'

Another look over those spectacles. 'It saves you from a lot of aggro.'

Lucy, cautious, held on. 'Francine had a visitor on Friday evening – a woman, apparently. You didn't happen to see who it was?'

'But I did. It was Madam. I saw her going up the steps to the flat. Very unusual. Madam doesn't go in for social calls. I said to myself, "It must be money!" And she was there for more than an hour so it was probably quite a lot of money.'

'You don't happen to remember when she left? I mean, was it dark? Have you any idea of the time?'

'If it was dark I wouldn't have seen her, would I? No, it was dusk – getting dark.'

It was obvious that Gew knew more than he was saying but he had picked up his stylus and seemed about to resume work. He was not the sort to respond to pressure and Lucy asked with a certain desperation, 'I don't suppose you know anything of the kind of tensions or fears or jealousies that might have led to the girl's death?'

Gew looked at her with a half-smile. 'We have plenty of all those in our "little community" as Daddy Archer likes to call it, but as far as I know none of us has yet reached the point where we might resort to murder. In fact, I've probably overstated the case against the girl simply because she happened to irritate me.'

Lucy risked: 'Exactly what is Mr Archer's role in the Guild?'

A quick frown. 'Hard to say. Daddy doesn't have much impact, but he's all right as long as Madam makes sure he gets his oat-bran for breakfast every morning. Keeps him regular, you know.'

Lucy grinned. 'You have a wicked streak, Mr Gew.'

'Well, my dear, you either laugh or you cry in this life. By the way, have you met Evadne?'

'Mrs Penrose?'

'The same. Evadne isn't one of the Guild. On the face of it she's just a spot of domestic help for the Archers, but don't under-estimate her; even Madam has to tread carefully where that little woman is concerned.'

Lucy was about to put another question but Gew stood up. 'No, that's it. I've said my piece and you must make what you can of it.'

An awkward cuss, but Lucy felt that she had no reason to complain. What Gew had said confirmed Lina's account of her visit to the dead girl, at least as to time and duration.

She left, but it was drizzling rain and she had stopped in the shelter of the doorway to consider her next move when Gew called after her, 'If you're thinking of the pottery for your next call you might tell Bob Lander to get a silencer for his blasted motorbike. Woke me up at six this morning.'

Consulting one of Lina's site plans, Wycliffe made himself familiar with the layout. On the west side of the stream there was Arthur Gew with his typography and engraving, Derek Scawn with his pottery, and Paul and Francine in the wood-carvers' shop. On the east side where Alice Field had her miniature crafts, there was the Archer house, and, on the rising ground behind, Emile Collis's studio and lodgings.

Wycliffe was intrigued by a substantial single-storied building, isolated and very close to the stream on the west side. On Lina's plan it was labelled 'The Guild-hall'. He noted the meticulous hyphenation and decided to take a look.

In contrast with the other buildings on the site, all of which owed something to their mining antecedents, it was clear that this little edifice had been purpose-built. Wycliffe walked around it, counting the sides, and after doing it twice, decided that there were, in fact, nine: a nonagon. Each side had a window of apparently stained glass so that it was not possible to see the inside. But the door was not locked and he went in.

The interior was dimly lit, theatrical, but in its way impressive. The stained-glass windows each displayed one of the signs of the Zodiac. Did they correspond with the nine members of the Guild? If so, any change of membership would be expensive. But closer examination revealed that they were not stained glass but made up of coloured papers, exquisitely cut and fitted together. Money might be a problem; time was not.

The ceiling was tent-shaped, a blue vault studded with stars, and the centre of the floor was occupied by a nonagonal table with nine chairs, each chair inscribed with the name of a Guild member and with his or her birth sign.

Like the 'reconstructions' of 'King Arthur's Hall' it was touched with both romance and absurdity.

Anyway Archer had been prepared and permitted to spend money on his fantasy and Wycliffe thought, with a certain sympathy, of the poor man struggling to reconcile all this with Lina's entrepreneurial ambitions. Squaring the circle might have been easier. And he wondered if it might be important to gauge the depth of Archer's commitment. Did it amount to an obsession?'

A trifling sound, and Wycliffe became aware that he was not alone. Evadne Penrose emerged from behind a screen on the other side of the room. Duster and whisk in hand she looked for all the world like a church-mouse intent on her self-imposed tasks. But there was nothing mouse-like about her manner. 'What do you want in here? There's nothing here for you!'

She came around the table to stand looking up at him.

Wycliffe's manner was conversational and placatory. He cut across her aggression. 'Do you go along with all this?'

Taken by surprise, she hesitated. 'It's Archer's way.'

'But as an astrologer yourself do you support him in his attempts to stand by the principles on which he founded the Guild?'

Evadne did not answer at once, then she said, 'It's not for me to say. I am not even a member of the Guild. But Archer is a man with a mission. He wants to see his Guild as a community in the service of the crafts but also in harmony with the Spheres. He knows well enough that as a commercial enterprise it must pay its way to survive but, after all, the monastic orders managed that sort of thing for long enough and some of them still do.'

Wycliffe reflected that ten years ago he had written this woman off as a rather kinky village gossip in a pinafore.

He wanted to keep her talking but realised that it would be easy to put her off. He risked an apparently casual comment: 'Archer strikes me as a dedicated man.'

'As I've said, he's a man with a mission. He sees himself as having been born a rather special person, with unique obligations. There's his name, and the fact that he was born under Sagittarius, the Archer, in the *ninth* house of the zodiac. Then there are the numerological implications in his name.'

'And they are?'

Evadne smiled. She had softened towards him. 'You should read it up, Mr Wycliffe. Archer's full name, believe it or not, is Francis Bacon Archer. His father wrote a book about Bacon. But the point is that in numerological terms the letters of his name add up to seventy-two, and seven plus two is nine. You see? Once again, the magically powerful number.' She broke off. 'And there is a lot more to it; most of it beyond me.'

She went on, 'At the moment Archer is having difficulty with his ideas on natal astrology. It has occurred to him that the planetary configurations which influence a child's future are those that apply at the actual time of birth, but science tells us that the genetic pattern is determined at the moment of conception. This worries him, and he is working desperately to reconcile the two.'

Wycliffe was intrigued. 'As an astrologer yourself, do Mr Archer's doubts trouble you?'

Evadne was totally dismissive. 'Not one bit! It's something on which we disagree. Archer is trying to apply logic to one of the magical arts, where the only rules that matter are the ones that work. They are their own justification.'

She brushed back a few grizzly hairs from her forehead. 'If there is anything good to be said of Aleister Crowley it is that he warned us against attributing objective reality to any such rules.'

Wycliffe felt that he was learning something of what made these people tick and he was loath to let go. 'You, like Archer, are, I believe, a Sagittarian. What is Lina's sign?'

A shrewd look. 'Lina is an Arian, Mr Wycliffe. What else? Impatient, born to lead. Certainly not to follow. Aries is the sign of the Ram.' The little brown eyes twinkled. 'Perhaps the battering ram.' She broke off. 'When were you born?'

'August the fifteenth.'

She nodded, 'A Leo . . . Not a bad sign for a policeman, but Leos have to guard against self-righteousness.' She squinted up at him. 'And on the physical side, watch out for your heart as you get older.'

She turned away. 'Well, I don't know about you, but I've got work to do.'

Evadne Penrose. A woman to be reckoned with.

Lucy was waiting for him in the shelter of the doorway. 'Collis next?'

'I suppose so, but I feel I've had enough already. However, onward and upward. We'll do him together.'

Collis had his studio and living quarters on the rising ground behind the Archers' house. It was a long, single-storied building with a number of windows, but it was impossible to see inside because the front of the building was raised on stilts to accommodate the slope.

They climbed the steps to the front door which stood open. Wycliffe knocked on the glass panel but there was no response. 'Let's go in.'

On the other side of a makeshift screen they found themselves in a large, square studio with cupboards and racks around the walls, the usual painter's gear and easels for work in progress. One of these was covered with a drape.

There was a door at each end and Wycliffe called out, but there was no response.

Lucy said, 'Look at these . . . '

Pinned to a large notice-board near the draped easel there were sketches, some in pencil, others in charcoal, all of the same girl and ranging from head only to the whole body in different postures.

Wycliffe said, 'Francine.' And he knew enough about drawing to recognise the economy of line and sureness of touch which spells talent.

'Are you looking for me?' A soft voice.

They had heard no sound but the door at one end of the room was now open and a man stood there. He was thin, very pale, with dark hair in tight curls which gave him a foreign look. Levantine? That was the word that came to Wycliffe's mind but he wasn't quite sure what it meant.

He made the routine introductions, holding out his warrant card as though it were a talisman. 'You are Mr Emile Collis?'

'Yes. I was resting and I must have fallen asleep. I know that you are here about Francine.'

'Is there somewhere we can talk?'

He looked vaguely around the studio. 'You'd better come in here.'

They followed him into an all-purpose room, shabbily furnished with an armchair and three or four other chairs, a table, a desk and a sort of dresser with an eclectic display of crockery and glass on its shelves.

Collis got them seated. 'You must forgive me; I am very distressed about Francine.'

'Have you any idea at all why someone might have done this to her?'

'No idea. It is horrible!'

'Did you know her well? Were you close to her?'

Collis looked up sharply but when he spoke his manner was hesitant. He seemed to be groping for the words that would best express his meaning. 'I don't know . . . I doubt if anybody was close to Francine. I was fascinated by her and, at the same time, wary. I had never before met anyone like her.'

'Can you enlarge on that?'

He looked at Wycliffe, frowning. 'It's very difficult. Francine was totally self-absorbed.' He hesitated. 'That sounds like a criticism and in a way I suppose it is. She was aggravating, but one didn't altogether resent her behaviour. Francine made her own rules and one accepted and respected them – even admired her for her courage and consistency, I suppose.' He broke off. 'Does that sound absurd?'

Wycliffe was impressed. 'No. I think you have described her as she was.'

'You knew her?'

'Many years ago.'

'Of course! You are the policeman who . . . She told me all about that. I assumed it was that which made her what she was.'

'From what you tell me, I don't think she'd changed.'

There was silence in the little room and it was Lucy Lane who broke it. 'You were painting her portrait?'

A self-deprecating smile. 'Oh, I've always wanted to be a portrait painter but one has to be a special sort of person; one has to establish a rapport with the sitter and that was beyond me. However, Francine was irresistible and I had to try.'

Wycliffe found this man interesting and the interview was turning into an informal chat. Time to get back to the nitty-gritty. He said, 'You will be asked to make a formal statement for the record, Mr Collis, but in the meantime there are one or two questions. Did you become emotionally involved with Francine?'

Collis hesitated. 'I suppose so. She fascinated me, I liked being with her— '

'Were you attracted sexually?'

'Sexually?' . . . A pause, then, 'No, sex didn't enter into our relationship and I can imagine Francine's reaction if I had approached her in that way.'

'It seems likely that the blocking of the flue outlet responsible for Francine's death was carried out after dark on Friday night. Were you out and about at any time during darkness that night?'

'Friday night? . . . I spent most of the evening framing.'

'Framing?'

'Yes. You may think it odd, but I do all the framing for the pictures we sell. I have a little workshop at the other end of this building. To do any picture justice it must be appropriately framed, if it is going to be framed at all. Anyway, I enjoy the work and I'm supposed to be good at it.'

'Did you go out at all on Friday night?'

Collis considered. 'As I recall, I packed up in the workshop at around ten and went for a walk over the moor. I— '

'Did you go anywhere near the wood-carvers' building?'

'No. I went out the back way from here, straight on to the moor. There is a footpath. I often take a walk before going to bed if the weather is anything like reasonable. I don't sleep well and I find it helps. I can't say exactly when I got back but I went to bed and slept until morning.'

'Do you know of any situation in which Francine was involved that might conceivably have led to her death?'

There was a moment for consideration before the answer came. 'No. It's true that Francine did not go about making friends – not in the Guild anyway, but I cannot see how any of these . . . these trifling antagonisms could have led to this.'

Wycliffe said, 'Just one more question and a very personal one. I gather from your colleagues that you have seemed to be a very worried man in recent weeks. Do your worries have any connection with Francine or with any events involving her?'

For the first time Collis's manner changed and he became brusque. 'My worries, as you call them, have nothing whatever to do with Francine. I have taken medical advice and I am told that being worried does not necessarily mean that one has specific cause for worry. I gather that it can be a psychological disorder which may be thought of as mental indigestion.' Collis sounded oddly spiteful.

And, for the time being, that had to be that.

On their way out Wycliffe stopped by the draped canvas. 'Is this your portrait?'

'Yes, but I would rather not show it to you at the moment.'

Outside Wycliffe said, 'Well?'

Lucy shook her head. 'I'm not falling for that one, sir, not at this stage.'

Chapter Five

Whit Monday continued

Lucy said, 'Shall we try the potter?'

Wycliffe looked at his watch. 'No. The Tributers'. It's lunch-time.'

As they drove to the Tributers' Kersey came through from the Incident Room on the car radio. 'The media are waking up, sir. Just three or four of them so far, including regional TV, but I'm afraid the murder of a girl in an art colony on a Cornish moor will go to their heads and it won't be long before they tumble to the "Quiet Virgin" link. Uniform are sending a couple of chaps to keep an eye on visitors as well as comings and goings in general.'

There were several cars and a camper-van parked near the Tributers' and among the group around the bar Wycliffe recognised two west-country journalists. Most of the tables were already occupied but Phyllis led them to one at the far end. 'There! I thought you might be in so I put a "reserved" on that one. You'll be nice an' quiet here.'

When they were settled, Lucy said, 'How do you do it? There must be something I've missed.'

A cheese salad for Lucy; the dish of the day for Wycliffe – roast chicken with cauliflower and chips. 'You've never lived, Lucy, until you've tasted Phyllis's chips.'

And almost in the same breath: 'There's Marsden and he's got the boy with him. I wonder what he's up to.'

Marsden had a table in a far corner by the bar and Paul Bateman was with him. Marsden raised a hand in salute.

Lucy said, 'From what you've told me he could be good for Paul.'

'You may be right at that.'

A few minutes later, after they had been served, Wycliffe said, 'This place is getting uncomfortably crowded. See who's just come in?'

The newcomer was a little woman, thin and angular, and she was almost totally enveloped in a coat made from the skin of some creature that seemed to have met its end in the middle of a moult.

Lucy, in a voice touched with awe, said, 'Ella Bunt! Just when I thought and hoped she'd got lost or something . . . And she's wearing that coat that smells of goat.'

Ella Bunt had been a notable if unlikely freelance crime reporter. With no apparent qualities or qualifications that fitted her for the job Ella had made a name for herself. As far as the police were concerned she had developed an uncanny knack of popping up with tradable bits of information which she would offer in return for privileged access. And she had a soft spot for Wycliffe. But in recent years she had faded out.

'She's seen us and she's coming over.'

On her way Ella collected a stray chair, brought it to their table, and, with a deep sigh, sat down. 'I thought I might find you here. What are you eating? . . . I'll have what you're having, Charlie.'

'Do you want something, Ella – other than food?'

'You need something other than food, Charlie. That's for sure.'

'And you've got it?'

'You tell me.'

Ella's meal arrived and she removed her coat to achieve greater freedom of action.

Wycliffe looked at the coat with distaste. 'That used to be part of your winter wardrobe, Ella.'

'Yes, but as I get older I feel the cold more. And it's a good coat. It cost real money once. Anyway, getting down to business, did your friend Marsden ever tell you about the Stylov Gallery?'

'I know that it was one of Lemarque's projects where they took commissions for paintings in the style of notable or famous painters.'

Ella drew her coat about her. 'Exactly. "Your friends will never know the difference." That was their line; and some of those paintings were sold on as the genuine article. They did a good job – canvas, stretchers, colours – all in period as you might say.'

'It was never proved that they were faking with intent to deceive.'

Ella was contemptuous. 'What the hell does that matter? You know it and I know it.'

'Are we coming to the point?'

Ella was rueful. 'I don't have to do this for you, Charlie. Anyway, the point is that there were two hack painters involved, and your Marsden was one of them.'

'I know that.'

'But you probably don't know that the other was Collis, though he wasn't Emile Collis then, he was Edward Collins, which could have been his real name for all I know. You notice that he kept the initials.'

Wycliffe was impressed. 'What you've told me could be very useful, Ella.'

'I'm glad you admit it. And, what's more, you'll find if you get CRO on the job that Edward Collins was sent down for two years in ninety-one and that the charge was forgery. He seems to have got off lightly.'

Wycliffe reflected that the past was catching up with a lot of people, including himself.

'Well, there it is, Charlie. I reckon that I've overpaid for this lunch and that you owe me.'

She turned to Lucy. 'I was in on it last time – as far as he would let me. He palmed me off on a widow-woman who was nutty about astrology, but she was more helpful than he imagined in other ways. I shall have to look her up if she's still around.'

And then to Wycliffe. 'You probably know that I'm semi-retired. Now I pick the odd case that attracts me and I'm rehashing some old stories with a book in mind.' She grinned. 'I'm mobile and fancy-free. The camper-van outside is mine and I share it with

Dickie Doyle who used to be my camera man. Dickie does the driving. Anyway, when I saw that you were back, picking away at an old sore, I couldn't resist offering a helping hand.'

And to Lucy Lane: 'What is it about him that makes women want to spoil him?'

Time passed in eating and reminiscence. Wycliffe said little and at last it was over; the party broke up.

Outside Lucy said, 'She gets to look more and more like an old witch. Can you really take her seriously?'

Wycliffe, sensitive about Ella, was curt. 'Editors do.'

'So where do we go from here?'

'I want to check up with Marsden but not while he's got Paul in tow. I think another visit to the Archers. With luck we might get Lina on her own, and now that we are better briefed . . . '

They were received in the Archers' sitting room – lounge? Anyway, good solid Dutch furniture, plenty of wood to polish; not very comfortable, but no smear or speck of dust anywhere. Lina had brought with her more than her baggage when she crossed the water.

There was a flower painting, elaborately framed, on the wall above the fireplace; probably worth a small fortune if it was what it seemed to be.

Lina said, 'You're looking at my painting. No, it's not the real thing, it's a copy of one of Huysum's which I did while I was still at the Rijks.'

She smiled. 'I'm rather proud of it.'

Lina seemed anxious to draw attention to her skill as a copyist and Wycliffe was duly complimentary.

Lina had rejected trousers in favour of a dress which she would regard as *de rigueur* in the circumstances: mauve with grey trimmings; decently sombre.

When they were seated she opened at once. 'I was past thirty when I met Archer; bored with the tedium of my work at the museum, and looking for a fresh start— '

But Wycliffe decided against allowing Lina to choose her

ground. 'Let's begin with the events of the past few days, and work back if we need to. You told me that you visited Francine in her flat last Friday evening. Will you tell me a little more about that and its possible implications?'

Diverted from her prepared script Lina was put off, but her recovery was swift. 'Emile told me that you had been asking about that visit. My reason for talking to Francine was simple. We needed to discuss her present and future role in the Guild.'

'Because she was considering a substantial investment.'

'Yes.'

'And, naturally, you wanted these discussions to be confidential.'

'Of course.'

Wycliffe asked, with an air of innocence, 'Your husband was not involved in this discussion?'

Lina shifted in her chair with a show of impatience. 'As I was about to explain earlier, Archer has very strong views about maintaining the Guild in its present form.' An indulgent smile. 'He is a romantic, Mr Wycliffe; a dear man, but not cut out for business. He wants to see the Guild as a small community of workers, mutually dependent, and wholly devoted to their respective crafts. Of course it has never been like that and never could be. Even Eric Gill, his role model, had a keen eye for business and rarely allowed his religion or, for that matter, his sex life to interfere. To survive we have to make a reasonable profit and ensure that our members are able to earn a decent living.'

Lina paused, considering her words. 'Another equally important factor for Archer is, of course, his preoccupation with astrology. I saw you coming out of the Nonagon.' A gesture. She seemed to be saying, You must realise what I'm up against! And she went on, 'Archer believes that there is great significance in his name and birth sign and that leads, along with other things, to his insistence that there must be nine of us.'

She spread her hands. 'You may think that this is nonsense but Archer, along with a great many others, takes it seriously, and I respect his beliefs. However, with or without Francine's investment it has been clear for some time that we must expand to survive and, inevitably, much of the present organisation by which Archer sets such store will have to go.'

Lina sat back in her chair as though to say, So there we are! Cards on the table.

Lucy Lane said, 'So any difficulties you had were with your husband rather than with Francine?'

An emphatic nod. 'Exactly! I needed time to discuss the business with Archer; above all to give him the chance to think again, and help him to see where our future must lie.'

Wycliffe, surfeited with the caring, affectionate, but frustrated wife, decided to give the proceedings more of an edge. 'Can you tell us how your purchases of pictures at auction in Amsterdam fits into the Guild's activities?'

It was clear that the question was not totally unexpected, but she managed a show of resentment. 'My purchases are an entirely private matter and have nothing to do with the Guild nor, I would have thought, with your inquiry.'

Wycliffe was equally blunt. 'I don't know what is relevant to my inquiry and what is not, but I intend to find out.'

Lina flushed. 'All right, I have nothing to hide. If it concerns you, I buy pictures in Amsterdam, backing my judgement, and, after cleaning and reframing where necessary, I sell them on. I get, as you English say, a kick out of it, and on balance I make a sufficient profit to justify my self-indulgence.'

'Did Francine raise this matter?'

'Yes, and she understood.' After a brief pause Lina went on, 'As far as Francine and I were concerned I have to say that we had a good deal in common. We both liked to have clear objectives and we were prepared to take risks to attain them. We were ready to place bets on the future.' She smiled, as though pleased with the simile. 'I enjoy pitting myself against the dealers and, like most gamblers, I hope one day to make what you might call "a killing".'

Wycliffe was thinking that in dealing with this woman it could become a question of who tripped up first.

The room looked out over the site and down the valley, with a glimpse of the sea. Drifting cloud shadows and patches of sunshine made ever-changing patterns on the face of the moor, and there were rain streaks on the window panes.

Wycliffe shifted his ground. 'If we assume that Francine's death was unrelated to the activities of the Guild then presumably it was a consequence of her personal relationships.'

Lina relaxed visibly. 'Yes, Mr Wycliffe, I think that is where you must look for an explanation of this terrible tragedy.'

'In our earlier conversation you mentioned her association with Paul Bateman, with Emile Collis and with the young man known as Blond Bob who works and lives with Scawn at the Pottery.'

Lina pulled her dress a little further down over her knees. 'Bob is something of a mystery but he is Scawn's problem and I interfere as little as possible.' A brief pause before she continued. 'I think that I've said all that I can about Francine and men. In her relations with them, as in everything else, what gave her satisfaction was the feeling of being in control; the sense of power.'

Lina paused before adding, 'Of course, it's not unlikely that in pursuing that line she got herself into some highly charged situations.' Another pause, then, 'But I know no more than I have told you.'

Lina was beginning to feel that she had won the round and her manner was confident.

But Wycliffe had not finished. 'You are a painter. Do you have a studio separate from the one used by Mr Collis?'

A quick smile. 'Yes, I have my own little studio upstairs. Do you wish to see it?' She was playing a game; her manner was almost flirtatious.

'Please.'

'Then you must come upstairs.'

Everywhere there was gleaming white paintwork setting off pile carpet in traditional colours, meticulously hoovered.

Lina's studio was in a former back bedroom. It was bare, spotlessly clean and innocent of clutter. An unframed painting rested on an angled board placed in a good light. There was a painter's trolley beside it.

Lina said, 'This is one of my recent purchases in Amsterdam. It has a scratch and I am doing a little minor restoration.' She added, 'That was my job in the museum.'

Her manner was teasing. 'This painting was a good buy, actually. A Paris street scene by the French Cortés – not the Spanish painter.' She turned to Wycliffe with a confiding smile. 'I hope to make a little on this one.'

She summed up: 'Well, Mr Wycliffe, we are honest practitioners of our craft, whatever you may suspect.'

Wycliffe was satisfied to leave Lina with her confidence intact. He said his thanks.

They were on their way along the passage to the stairs when she pushed open a door that was already ajar. 'While you are here, you might like a word with Archer. This is his room – a little different from mine, as you can see.'

Archer was seated at a table by the window, his back to the door. He turned in his chair, looking at them over his spectacles, none too pleased at the interruption.

'Mr Wycliffe would like a word, dear.'

All the available wall space was covered with what appeared to be star charts. Books spilled over from shelves on to heaps on the floor. A painter's easel and trolley stood apparently neglected in one corner, and the table at which Archer worked was littered with papers and books open for reference.

There was a single bed against one wall.

Lina said, 'Archer has all but given up painting in order to pursue his astrological researches and, as you know, he has recently recruited Evadne Penrose to help him. It seems that she is also very knowledgeable about such things.'

Archer composed himself. Initially resenting the interruption, he was not prepared to miss a chance to spread his gospel. And Wycliffe was well aware that the situation was of Lina's deliberate contrivance. Mere mischief? Or with some serious intent?

Archer was under way. 'I believe that our theory of natal astrology has to be recast in the light of scientific knowledge that was not available to our ancestors. I refer, of course, to the science of genetics.'

Archer shifted his chair to face his audience. 'The study of genetics, beginning with Mendel, and enormously developed since, has made it clear that our characteristics are, in terms of the actual physical process, determined not at the time of birth but at the moment of conception. In my view it must therefore be at that moment that the planetary influences make themselves felt.'

There was a pause awaiting some comment from Wycliffe and he did his best to sound intelligent. 'And that, I suppose, throws the whole system about nine months out of gear?'

An emphatic nod and a quick smile. 'As our prime minister said in another context, we have to think the unthinkable. Either all our interpretations are totally wrong or we are associating those interpretations with the wrong configurations of the planets. For example, the characteristics which we now associate with the configuration in Sagittarius – November/December – may in fact be determined by the situation in Aries – March/April.'

Archer removed his spectacles and stroked his silky beard. 'It is a revolutionary idea, Mr Wycliffe, and for me, a very disturbing one.'

Wycliffe was silent but Lina was quick off the mark. 'And in my view a good time to make those changes in the Guild which are desirable, even if they are inconsistent with astrological principles which you are discarding anyway.'

But Archer was emphatic. 'Oh, no! Oh, no. One doesn't throw away an old coat until one is quite sure that the new one fits. I am a long way from that situation at the moment.' And he turned his back on them as a peremptory sign of dismissal.

Back in the corridor Lina's manner was almost conspiratorial. 'You see? Never mind; we shall get there in the end.'

Downstairs they were shown off the premises with a display of apparent good will from both sides.

Lucy asked, 'Why were we treated to all that?'

Wycliffe said, 'I hoped that you were going to tell me. The point she was making was pretty obvious but I wish I knew why she troubled to make it.'

'You saw the bed in his room.'

'One could hardly miss it. Anyway, we've left Lina in the right mood. The last thing I want is to have her getting scared without us knowing exactly what she's scared of. We want her to feel pleased with herself and at the moment she doesn't need encouragement.'

'It sounds Machiavellian.'

'You think so? I only hope that we can keep up with her.'

'You didn't mention Collis's record.'

'No, we need something up our sleeve.'

Wycliffe looked at his watch. It was four o'clock and still Whit Monday.

A little more than thirty hours ago he had been lounging in the Watch House garden. Helen was weeding, Macavity was asleep at his feet. It was hard to believe. His mobile had put an end to all that.

A girl had been murdered.

Now he knew the girl was Francine Lemarque. As in a dream he was meeting familiar faces in a fresh context and it looked as though threads from the past had been interwoven with others into a new and ugly pattern.

He turned to Lucy Lane. 'I need to get home this evening, Lucy.'

'You're thinking of your interview in the morning?'

'Yes.'

There was a moment or two of silence, then Lucy said, 'We all hope that you will be there to see us through, sir.'

'See you through? I don't understand.'

Lucy was looking straight in front of her. 'You might be tempted to pack it in – and who could blame you? But we just hope that you won't.'

He was surprised, taken off balance, and all he could find to say was, 'Thank you.'

Lucy changed the subject. 'How do we go tomorrow?'

'We are neglecting the potter and his assistant, Lander.'

'You want me to make a start?'

Wycliffe hesitated. 'Concentrate on Lander. Send for him and get him talking. I would rather we tackled Scawn together.'

Lucy got the message.

Wycliffe was looking across the stream towards the wood-carver's workshop. 'I wonder if Paul is there.'

'Shall we find out?'

'I'd like to tackle him alone, Lucy.'

'You don't think that you may be letting sentiment run away with you in this case?'

About to take offence, he changed his mind. 'Of course I am, and so would you in similar circumstances.'

Lucy grinned. 'You may be right at that.'

'When I've talked to Paul I shall look in on Marsden. Then homeward.'

Lucy said, 'Good luck!'

The door of the wood-carver's workshop was open and inside Paul was using a tiny gouge on a plaque with a floral design. He turned to face Wycliffe, dropped the gouge, and stood with his back to the bench, waiting for what was to come. He looked haggard and ill.

'I want to talk to you, Paul. Do you think we could sit down?'

Paul pointed to a couple of trestles. 'We don't have chairs.'

'I'm not talking as a policeman, and we are alone. I want to find whoever killed Francine and so do you. If you tell me what is in your mind – your private thoughts about what has happened – I will promise that nothing you say will recoil on you in any way.'

There was a silence and when Paul finally spoke, words came slowly. 'It took me a very long time to realise that Francine would never enter into a stable relationship with anybody. I only really understood it after she moved into the flat upstairs . . . Until then I had always hoped.'

Another silence, but Wycliffe was content to wait.

'I was . . . I was disappointed – hurt, I suppose. I knew that my attachment was too strong to face any break. If all I could have was her company at work, and perhaps her companionship sometimes outside of work, I would settle for that. We'd been through so much together that for me the idea of separation . . . ' He left the sentence unfinished.

Such total commitment must be very nearly unique and Wycliffe could not help wondering what the future held for Paul without the girl.

'Were you jealous of her association with other men?'

He considered before answering. 'I don't think I was. They had less of her than I had.' He shifted his position on the trestle. 'Being put away changed Fran and, God knows, that's not surprising. She came out determined to get her own back on life but I don't think you can do that; you can only get your own back on people.'

'You knew that she had inherited money and that she was proposing to invest it in the Guild?'

'I heard the talk but that didn't affect me one way or the other.'

'Can you suggest any reason why anyone would have wanted to murder Francine? Can you think of anyone who hated or feared her enough to plan and carry out such a cold-blooded crime?'

Paul shook his head. 'It's beyond me . . . In the night I have difficulty in persuading myself that it could have happened. I can almost believe that it was a bad dream.'

Wycliffe said, 'I saw you with Marsden. I think he might be helpful to you.'

'He is. He's been very understanding. He showed me his painting of Francine and he's promised to give it to me. It's wonderful! I mean it's Francine *before* . . . ' There were tears in his voice and in his eyes. 'To think that I didn't even know of its existence . . . And Marsden talks about Fran as though he understood her in a way I think nobody else did.' He added, after a pause, 'Not even me.'

Just time, before he left, to tackle Marsden. Wycliffe drove himself.

The sky was overcast and a thin drizzle kept the screen-wipers busy. Gloom! But it was very mild. Good weather for growing Cornishmen and cabbages, but Wycliffe did not quite fit into either category.

The light was on in Marsden's living room but there was no music. Wycliffe banged on the door and it was opened by Marsden. 'You! I've got a visitor.'

'Good! Now you've got two.'

Evadne Penrose was installed in one of the Windsor chairs by the fireplace with Percy stretched out at her feet. For once Evadne was caught off balance.

'I came to bring Hugh up to date. He so hides himself away in this place that he never hears anything unless someone takes the trouble to tell him.'

Wycliffe felt he owed Evadne something but policemen rarely pay their debts, and he gave her no encouragement. She went on, 'Hugh and I have been neighbours more or less for twelve years.'

Put off by the continuing absence of any response, she stood up. 'Well, I've done my duty so I shall leave you to talk.'

She wore a navy-blue gabardine mac, which looked as though she might have had it since her schooldays.

Marsden, unusually silent, saw her off. When he came back, and had closed the door, he said, 'You can never tell with Evadne. There's more to her than you'd think.'

'What did she want?'

'She told you.'

'Interesting!'

'You think so? I might ask what business it is of yours, anyway; but I won't. Evadne gathers what she can where she can.'

Wycliffe took the chair Evadne had vacated and refused to be diverted from her visit. 'Perhaps Evadne knew that your acquaintance with Collis goes further back, and that you know a good deal more about him than you've admitted to me. For example, that he worked with you in the Stylov Gallery racket, not as Emile Collis, but as Edward Collins, and that he's done time for forgery since then.'

Marsden was recovering his poise. 'So you've tumbled to it, or somebody's tipped you off. But get this straight, I'm not your snout waiting to grass up my acquaintances, past or present.'

'But you're as anxious as I am to find the killer of Francine.'

Marsden turned to Wycliffe with something of his old style. 'I'm as dry as a boot-jack so what about a glass of our Phyllis's elixir?'

When they were settled, Marsden went on, 'Look at it my way

for once. The whole art trade, as far as painting is concerned, is an elaborate scam. Somebody turns up with a painting of bloody sunflowers. "Is it an unknown Van Gogh?" he asks with bated breath and twitching fingers. Well, if there's a chance in hell, it will eventually get to be brooded over by the art gnomes in London, in Paris or New York. And, in due time, after taking into consideration many things not in the least relevant to the picture itself, they will make their Olympian pronouncement.'

Marsden paused to take a great gulp from his glass. 'And as a result, this bit of canvas with paint on it will be worth either ten million or five hundred to its owner. And even the five hundred will need a bit of luck. And, the poor bugger who painted it – or didn't – shot himself in despair more than a century ago.'

'So? Are we going to get to the point?'

This time Marsden only sipped his beer. 'We're already there. The whole bloody business is a stupid but legal racket with a lovely fat profit for some. Well, if there's still anything in it for my old mate, Collins or Collis, or whatever he's calling himself at the moment, I'm not going to start nit-picking over his morals.'

'You didn't hesitate to point me in the direction of Lina and her Amsterdam trips. It was obvious that you suspected some jiggery-pokery there that was almost certain to involve Collis.'

'And this is the thanks I get. No, you are investigating the murder of a girl for whom I had a lot of time and, as you pointed out earlier, I want the bastard who did it caught, locked up and the key lost. Whoever he or she turns out to be.'

'How did Collis get into the Archer set-up?'

'It was through me, actually. Lina offered me the job but I'm not joining any bloody production line so I passed her on to my former mate. He'd just been let out after doing fifteen of his twenty-four months inside, and he was down on his luck. Lina took to him – he appeals to a certain type of woman – but there was more to it than that.'

'Did she know of his conviction?'

Marsden grinned. 'What do you think? Lina didn't go in for any pig in a poke. That was half the attraction.'

'Are you saying that he might be copying her Amsterdam purchases and that she flogs them as originals?'

Marsden pouted. 'I don't know. I suppose it's possible. But not all of them, that's for sure. She'd never get away with it. In any case, they're not really in a class that makes forgery worthwhile. It would have to be the odd one now and again, carefully selected and even more carefully placed. I gather that she rarely buys anything without good evidence of provenance. I suppose she could be really naughty and flog the fake with the provenance and let the original speak for itself. Even so there can't be a fortune in it but it might pay for her trips back home and leave a bit over. Though, knowing our Lina, she might even be doing it for kicks.'

Wycliffe sighed. 'And Francine is dead.'

'Yes, and that gets me where it hurts, but I can't believe that her death has anything to do with any picture fiddle they may be working. It's a jigsaw and there must be more than one way of putting it together, but you're supposed to be good at that.'

'Another thing. Derek Scawn – anything on him?'

Marsden frowned. 'A potter. They're a rum lot, neither fish, flesh nor fowl. Anyway Scawn is well out of my class – he's got brains. Or so they tell me.'

'What do you know about this chap they call Blond Bob – Robert Lander?'

'I know nothing about him. He was brought in by Lina, ostensibly to keep Scawn happy, but Lina isn't the sort to do anything unless there's something in it for her.' Marsden yawned. 'It's nearly tea time and what with one thing and another I haven't had my afternoon nap.'

'Poor you.'

Marsden saw him off. 'Don't let it get you down.'

Back at the site DCs Curnow and Thorne were in the caravan working through their formal interviews. Lucy was nowhere to be seen.

Wycliffe set off for home. By the time he reached the Hayle bypass he had left the mist and drizzle behind and when he arrived at the Watch House in the early evening, the sun was shining, the air was still and the waters of the estuary were like the proverbial mill pond.

He found such evenings mildly depressing; they reminded him of Bishop Heber's hymn, with 'all the saints casting down their golden crowns around the glassy sea'. As a child, the hymn had put him off quiet summer evenings. And heaven too.

Helen had made a prawn salad and, as part of his continuing musical education they listened to Sibelius's Seventh. Pleasantly gloomy, and in tune with his mood. Anyway, no sonic shocks.

They went to bed early and read. Before they settled down Helen asked, 'How do you feel about tomorrow?'

'I've decided to soldier on for a while. See how things go.'

'Good. I don't think you are quite ready for your clock, or whatever, just yet.'

'But if she thinks she's going to run me— '

'She'll be making a big mistake. I know, I've tried it. Now, kiss me good-night and go to sleep.'

And Wycliffe went to sleep, wondering at the number of odd-shaped hours which somehow slot together to make a day.

Chapter Six

Tuesday morning

In the morning, uneasy in his mind, and irritated because he was uneasy, Wycliffe's mood was not improved by the breakfast-time news on the radio: 'Investigations are continuing in the case of the young woman murdered on Saturday night at a craft colony near St Ives in Cornwall. The police have acknowledged that the victim was Francine Lemarque who, ten years ago, was herself convicted of the murder of Gerald Bateman, a rising political figure of the time, and her natural father— '

Wycliffe said, 'That's all I needed.'

'It was sure to come out.'

'You think that helps?'

He queued his way into the city inhaling his ration of exhaust fumes. For most of those stuck in the traffic it was back to work after a holiday weekend. Not for him. He arrived at police headquarters resolved to be difficult, and at nine-fifteen he presented himself outside the padded door. Queenie, the grey-haired and revered guardian of the sanctum, said, 'Go on in. She's waiting for you.'

'Oh, Charles! Do come in and sit down. I've been looking forward to this.' Smiling. She looked trim and youthful in her uniform.

A brief review of his file, then, 'I assume you're not planning to walk out on us? If you are, I hope I can change your mind, so listen to me first.

'You must know better than most how well Bertram Oldroyd ran this force and I understand that he did it largely by letting his heads of departments run their own shows as long as they stuck to the accepted rules of policing and got results. I've no intention of trying to change that.' A quick smile. 'I want to make it clear that if you sometimes choose to do the job of a DI or a DS, or, for that matter, of a beat copper, you won't hear any criticism from me as long as you continue to get the results the Force has come to expect from you, and that your administrative responsibilities are not neglected.'

Jane Elizabeth Sawle in Bertram Oldroyd's chair. It took some getting used to but she was putting him in the mood to try.

'I intend to make changes but they will be mostly concerned with administration. I want to reduce paperwork and so get more of our people away from their desks and out on the ground. I can see you saying to yourself, "She'll learn!" and you may be right, but I've got one or two ideas and I'm going to try. Much of our trouble comes from lawyers in the CPS and the Courts making jobs for themselves. Well, I'm a lawyer and that must be good for something.'

She laughed. 'All right so far? Now, I'm obviously interested in budgets – I have to be – and here again I think it may be possible to divert funds away from the offices and into practical policing with more men on the ground.'

Wycliffe had been wrong-footed but he was not going to be smothered in honeyed words. He had come prepared to say his piece and he said it.

The ensuing exchange, and it soon became a vigorous one, lasted for more than an hour and ended with, 'By the way, I hate being addressed as Ma'am, Charles. I have two names and of the two I prefer Jane, so when there are no junior ranks present I suggest we can dispense with Ma'am and use our first names.'

Wycliffe found himself back in Queenie's office feeling as though he had got there by parachute. All too good to be true? Perhaps. But time would soon tell.

Queenie, who had never hitherto been known to express any opinion about anything, remarked, 'She takes you that way, but we'll get used to it.'

He went through to his own office. Diane, his personal assistant, was there, sorting through the mail.

It was an odd feeling; he seemed to have been away for a long time.

'Well?' Diane was in her forties; she had been with him for more than twenty years and in private they no longer stood on ceremony.

'I think we shall survive.'

'You'll stay?'

'I'll give it a go.'

'Good! Hadn't you better ring Helen? . . . I'll leave you to it.'

Helen said, 'So I'm not going to have you here mooning around all day in carpet slippers. Seriously, love, I only want what you want, but I don't think you're ready for the handshake just yet.'

Helen. Bless her!

It was still only half-past eleven when Wycliffe was driving over the road bridge which, with the railway, the ferries and the airways, keeps Cornwall in touch with and at the mercy of the English. The sun had broken through the morning cloud and it looked like being a pleasant day. Oddly, his thoughts revolved around two clever and very different women, Lina Archer and Jane Sawle.

He sometimes wondered how different the Western world would have been if women had come into their own a hundred years earlier.

Better?

A good question, which he sometimes answered one way and sometimes the other. Eve, with the serpent in the garden, should have been a lesson to all mankind but it took a lot of learning, and Islam preferred to overlook it altogether. Or perhaps the Muslims overreacted.

He decided to put in an appearance at the Incident Room before going on to the Guild site.

Kersey was there at his table, working through reports from HQ which had been faxed through. None of them had anything to do with the case in hand but somebody had to deal with routine and, with a sense of guilt, Wycliffe recalled his licence from the new chief to stay out of line: 'If you sometimes choose to do the job of a DI or a DS, or a beat copper . . . '

All very well for him, but Kersey seemed to harbour no grievance.

Wycliffe did his best to reassure him about the new management.

Kersey said, 'So she's not going to be on our backs. That's something if she sticks to it. You'll stay on?'

'I shall stay long enough to see how it works out.'

'Well, that's what we've been waiting to hear. I don't have to say that the team will be pleased.'

Coming from Kersey that was a great deal.

'Any news of Lander?'

'He's back. I heard only just before you came in. Lucy is handling it.'

Delegation. Wycliffe had quite a good vocabulary but this was one word he had never really learned.

Kersey went on, 'Franks' report on the autopsy arrived. Nothing new that I can see. The statements are coming in. Nothing startling so far.' He yawned, patting his gaping mouth inadequately. 'And incidentally the inquest on the girl has been opened and adjourned. Anyway, it's lunchtime, so let's forget it for half an hour.'

Wycliffe was temporarily won over and they ate canteen sandwiches washed down with coffee from the machine.

'I think I'd better get out there.'

Kersey's grin said it all.

Wycliffe drove to Mulfra. As always, he felt that lift of the spirit as the car topped the rise outside Eagle's Nest. He could see the little village with its church tower below him, dwarfed by that vast spread of moor, and cliffs and sea. The sun still shone, but not with that Mediterranean monotony and intensity. There were clouds, white and puffy, that knew their places in the changing pattern of the sky as though they had been choreographed.

Perhaps, when we do retire . . . But on second thoughts, it's a long way from a Marks and Spencer's.

He arrived at the Guild site to find Lucy Lane in the police caravan about to interview Lander, and decided to sit in.

'Mr Robert Miles Lander, sir.' And to the young man. 'This is Detective Superintendent Wycliffe. At this stage we are interviewing everybody who had any connection with the dead girl, gathering as much information about her as possible. There is no implication of guilt or suspicion. You understand?'

'Of course.'

Lander was probably in his early thirties, tall and muscular, but his face was round and his features had an unfinished look, lumpy like a clay mask awaiting its final moulding. With his straight blond hair and pudding-basin cut, he looked like a vastly overgrown child.

Lucy said, 'Mr Lander has been away. He left yesterday morning and returned today.'

Lander was apologetic. 'I should have let you know but I was worried. I had a message from my father to say that my mother was unwell. She gets periodic attacks of migraine and father gets worked up. She's all right now.'

It was clear to Wycliffe that Lucy was uneasy, and he was puzzled. He decided to leave the questioning to her.

'How well did you know Francine?'

A frown. 'Hard to say. As you know, I live with Derek Scawn and Francine worked and lived a couple of doors away. She looked in occasionally and we seemed to get on. Derek liked her. In the same way I would drop in at wood-carving when they weren't too busy. It was all very casual.'

'Have you been to her flat?'

'Three or four times.'

'Was your relationship a close one?'

'You are asking me if it included sex. It did not.' Lander hesitated before adding, 'I'm not interested in women in that way.'

'Did you see her on the day she died?'

'No, I did not.'

Wycliffe asked, 'Did she confide in you at all?'

'She told me that she had come into money, and that she was negotiating with Lina about investing in the Guild.'

'What was your opinion about that?'

'I didn't have one. It was none of my business.'

'Did she talk to you about her past?'

'Yes, quite early on. I thought she was making it up just to be interesting.' He looked at Wycliffe. 'Some girls are like that. Then of course I heard it from others.'

Unusually, Lucy cut across Wycliffe's line of questioning. 'How long have you lived with Mr Scawn?'

'Nearly three years.'

'Are you related?'

'We are cousins twice removed.'

'So you have known him all your life?'

'No.' Hesitation. 'It was only by chance that I discovered our relationship.'

'Was that before or after you came to live with him?'

'It was after.'

Wycliffe was puzzled by Lucy's line of questioning but it was clear that Lander was becoming unsettled so he held his peace. Then, to his surprise, Lucy wound up the interview.

'Well, that will be all for the moment, Mr Lander. In common with the others who knew the dead girl at all well you may be required to make a formal statement later.'

Lander too seemed bewildered. 'I can go?'

'Of course. Thank you for your time.'

When he was gone Wycliffe said, 'What was all that about? I realise that I blundered in when I shouldn't have done.'

'You could say that. It was awkward but you couldn't have known. The point is that David Wills, the local DS, spotted Lander and told me just before the interview that he'd come across him before. It goes back several years to when Dave was in uniform and stationed in Exeter. Lander is a case of once seen never forgotten, and Dave remembers him being brought up on a drugs charge which was thrown out for lack of evidence. Dave wasn't directly involved but he's going to follow it up.'

'Interesting.'

'I thought so, and it seemed just as well not to put too much pressure on Lander in the meantime.'

'I shall eat humble pie.'

'Not too much. I don't want you getting indigestion.'

Half-past three, and Wycliffe said, 'So where do we go from here?'

Lucy suggested, 'Collis?'

'I'm not ready for him yet. Let's see what Scawn has to say for himself.'

The pottery building was on a larger scale than any of the others. The workshop was fitted with folding doors with a wicket. And parked nearby was a well-groomed Volvo, two or three years old.

Inside there was a bake-house warmth. The light was dim and a red eye glowed on one of the kilns. As their vision accommodated they could see work-benches, and at least two potters' wheels. There was a background smell of damp clay and on shelves lining the walls there were pots of different shapes and sizes in various stages of embryonic development.

A group of finished pots, presumably ready for packing, stood on a side table. Wycliffe was impressed by the brilliance of the colours and by the moulded figures of mythical beasts which twined round and clung to the elegant curves of some of them. For Wycliffe, uninspired by Helen's taste for the severities in colour and form of the Leach school, these pots were a revelation.

'May I help you?' A cultured voice from the far end, and a figure emerged from the gloom. 'Derek Scawn. You must be from the police.'

Introductions over, Scawn went on, 'I gather you've been talking to Robert. We were about to start unloading one of the kilns but he's just gone into Penzance to catch up on our shopping. We'd better go upstairs to my living quarters.'

Scawn was long, lean, dark and fiftyish, with a strong bone structure. Wycliffe found his steady gaze disturbing; he seemed to be looking through one, as though at some more distant object of greater interest.

But his manner was friendly, even chatty. 'I expect you're here to talk about Francine.'

He led the way to the back of the workshop and up a flight of stairs. At the top they were in a large room with a window on to the moor. White walls, Japanese prints, bookcases, a polished stripped-oak floor and Chinese rugs. At one end a vintage word processor shared a table with a few books and a bundle of typescript. No pots, Scawn or Leach, to be seen.

A silver-point Siamese padded about in restless disdain, while another achieved a complex yet elegant posture attending to its more intimate toilet.

When they were seated Wycliffe said, 'So Lander was called away unexpectedly.'

'Oh, yes, a telephone call yesterday from his father. Some family crisis. They live in Devon – Honiton, I think it is. I probably have the address somewhere. He visits them regularly, whenever he can get away.'

'I gather he has a motorcycle.'

'Yes – *very* useful in these lanes and on the moorland roads. As I said just now, he's off doing our shopping at the moment.'

Wycliffe was putting the onus on Scawn to do the talking, and the potter went on, 'Robert has kept me up to date with your investigation. The young woman came here several times and I believe Robert visited her at the wood-carving shop.'

Wycliffe, casual, asked, 'Do you see much of the other Guild members here?'

'Not a lot. Collis looks in at the pottery occasionally, and sometimes up here. He and Robert seem to have interests in common.' A ghost of a smile. 'Archer himself is a fairly regular visitor. As you probably know by now he has made a study of natal astrology and he comes here to share his thoughts.'

Wycliffe, anxious to keep the man talking, said, 'At the moment he seems to have got himself into a logical tangle concerning conception and birth in relation to astrological prediction.'

Scawn stooped to lift one of the cats on to his knees, and stroked it into purring contentment. 'Archer's tangle arises from his insistence on confusing two totally different systems of thought: the concept of cause and effect, which has been the keystone of Western science, and the idea of meaningful coincidence which underlies classical Chinese philosophy. Of course it is the latter which provides what logical framework there is for the study of astrology. Certain events "go together", and that is that. No point in further discussion— '

Scawn broke off. 'But is it really Archer that you have come to talk about?'

Wycliffe's response was brusque. 'I've come to talk about anyone and anything that may seem relevant to my investigation. I have to discover the motive for Francine's murder, and to do that I need to know as much as possible about the people with whom she was in regular contact.'

Scawn was not intimidated. Still with a hint of amusement in his voice he said, 'And I suppose one possibility is that poor Archer could have done it to secure the future of his Guild against a predator from within.' A thin smile. 'Interesting! I must admit that the thought occurred to me but I can't really see him going that far even in defence of his Guild.'

Wycliffe let that pass and Scawn went on, 'We all make what we can of the flux in which we find ourselves. We search for patterns in its swirls and eddies, and when we think we've found one we try to pin it down, to give it permanence. We theorise and rationalise about it, and say, "This is how things are." '

A broad gesture. 'Then, according to our bent, we call what we have contrived philosophy, science, religion, art or whatever.'

Scawn paused and looked directly at Wycliffe. 'In those circumstances, who am I to pass judgement on Archer's ideas or anyone else's?'

Wycliffe decided to go along with the whimsy. 'You've told us that Francine visited here and that you talked to her. What was your impression? If you like, what would you say was her selection from the eddies and whirlpools of the flux?'

Scawn grinned. 'A good question! And I need to think . . . Yes, well . . . I would say that Francine had chosen the most baffling and frustrating of them all, the illusion of individuality, of seeing in the flux her own image.' A pleased nod. 'Yes, and what is more she seems to have believed that she could isolate herself from the flow, and even attack it.'

Wycliffe was intrigued, and decided to play along. He waited until Scawn resumed: 'Freud believed that most of us are scared of our own individuality. We take refuge in the Family, the Team, the Party, the Church or the Mob. But Francine delighted in her self-hood and deliberately set out to exploit it . . . A risky business.'

Wycliffe was silent and Lucy, unsure whether this was her cue but anxious to find firmer ground, decided to risk it. 'Coming back to Robert Lander, what exactly is his position here?'

Scawn, momentarily wrong-footed, recovered. 'Officially he is my apprentice and he is a promising one, with the makings of a good potter.'

'Do you know anything of his background?'

'Very little. No more than he has told me in casual conversation.'

Wycliffe took up the thread. 'We have to make detailed inquiries concerning everyone who was in any way involved with the dead girl.'

'Naturally; and you may well find that Robert does not have an unblemished record. He is much given to blending fiction with fact and he does it so successfully that he is often unsure which is which.'

'And that doesn't trouble you?'

'Not in the least. Let me say at once that Robert has no streak of viciousness in his make-up. If you *know* him, you make allowances for his foibles, and he is harmless. At the same time he is a valuable companion: he is willing to work, he interests himself in those things that interest me and he is an excellent housekeeper. Without him this place would sink into squalor.'

'I understand that he is a relative of yours?'

An indulgent smile. 'That is one of his fantasies. He took the trouble to find out all he could about my background then came up with fictitious relatives of his own and fitted them together. It's just one of Robert's little games. Quite harmless.'

'And you let him get away with it?'

'Why not?' Another smile. 'God, or whatever, lets me think I've won sometimes.'

'How long have you known him?'

Scawn frowned. 'A couple of years, something like that. Lina realised that I needed help in the pottery and she sent him along for a trial period. He had had no experience but he was quick to learn.'

'What does he live on? Does he have anything apart from his wages?' Lucy again, feeling on firmer ground.

A quick look from Scawn. 'No private means, as far as I know. Robert works with me and, if you like, for me, so I make sure that he is provided for and though he does not know it, that will continue should anything, as we so coyly put it, "happen to me".'

Wycliffe tried one more throw. 'Do you have any ideas concerning Francine's murder?'

Scawn considered. 'Not really. I believe that she intended to work her way into the administration of our little community.' Scawn smiled as he said this. 'To work her way in and eventually, perhaps, take over from Lina.'

He added after a pause, 'You must realise, I'm sure, that friend Archer only operates under licence from his dear wife.'

Wycliffe had one more point. 'You know of Lina's visits to Amsterdam?'

'Of course. There's no real secret about them: she's Dutch and she goes back home.'

'And the pictures she buys and sells on?'

Scawn frowned. 'Lina is careful with her money and she probably does it to cover the expenses of her trip.'

For the moment it seemed that all had been said that needed to be at this stage, and Wycliffe stood up. 'Perhaps you will allow us to take a look at Lander's room.'

Scawn looked surprised. 'His room?' . . . Then, 'In the circumstances I suppose that is reasonable.'

The room was small but it looked out over the moor and despite the mist there was an illusion of space. A bedsitter, but with no resemblance to the traditional bachelor pad. The little room was plain, obsessively neat and tidy, with an institutional flavour. Wycliffe went to the bookshelves. A diverse collection of paperback novels kept company with books on history, science and philosophy, with language tutors in French and German, and an ageing set of the *Encyclopaedia Britannica*.

Scawn said, 'I believe that Robert thinks knowledge is power and so he does his best to get it.'

As they walked away from the pottery the mist was lifting and the moor slowly emerged in contour and colour. A few minutes later they could see the sea.

Wycliffe said, 'What did you make of Scawn?'

'Would you settle for a magnetic personality?'

Wycliffe grinned. 'It'll do for the present but I doubt if we've finished with him yet.'

'I'm glad to hear it.'

'Why, in particular?'

'I'd hate to see a Detective Super, still in fair condition, being carried away by the flux.'

Wycliffe could think of no apt reply to that, so he said nothing.

They crossed the stream. A post van was parked outside the Archer house, and the postman was delivering mail; a reminder that in the larger world life went on.

Wycliffe said, 'Our next port of call?'

Lucy said, 'What about Collis?'

'Yes, I think so. At least we can hear what he has to say about Lina's trips to Amsterdam.'

They made their way around the Archer house. Collis was in his studio, wearing a grey paint-stained overall which almost reached the floor, working on a beach scene. He was unwelcoming.

'I realise that our interruption may be troublesome but we need to talk to you.' Wycliffe was brusque.

Without a word, Collis wrapped a strip of polythene around the bristles of his brush and dropped it into a jar.

'We'd better sit down, I suppose.'

He led the way into his living room, and when they had found

103

seats he waited like a man about to be sentenced. He was in a bad way; the change in such a short time was remarkable. His movements were unsteady, sometimes exaggerated, and a tic affected one side of his mouth.

Drugs? Wycliffe wondered.

The first question took him by surprise. 'Do you know that Lina spent an hour with Francine in her flat on Friday evening?'

'No, but I can imagine there were matters they needed to discuss.'

Lucy asked, 'Money matters?'

A quick look. 'Probably.' He hesitated, then made up his mind. 'You must know that Francine had come into money and that there was a proposal that she should invest it in the Guild as capital for an expansion of the business. It was supposed to be very hush-hush but there's no point in that now. However, an investment of that kind would have required changes in our constitution so there was a lot to discuss.'

He spoke in a low voice; he was lucid, but it was obvious that he was under great strain.

Wycliffe spoke more gently. 'I'm sorry to press you on matters which may seem to have nothing to do with Francine's death, but you must understand that we have to look at every possibility.'

'I suppose so.'

'I gather that Francine was going around the workshops asking questions, and prying into details of how the present system affected different people. Did this upset some members of the Guild?'

'Yes, you could say that. Francine wasn't always as diplomatic as she might have been. But I can't see how that could be in any way connected with what has happened.'

'Unless she stumbled on something of real importance that she was not intended to know.'

Collis burst out, 'You are being melodramatic. To suggest that there was some secret that cost Francine her life is nothing less than absurd!'

Wycliffe was patient. 'But Francine was murdered and there

must have been a motive. Does it seem to you more likely that her death was a result of tangled personal relationships?'

For a moment Collis looked at Wycliffe in silence, then his features contorted as in a child about to burst into tears. He almost shouted, 'I don't know! I really don't know! What is the use of asking me these questions? You must know by now that Francine was a difficult young woman with a deeply distressing past. I suppose you could say that she wanted relationships without commitment. A lot of people do, but they are not murdered because of it.'

Collis slumped back in his chair, apparently exhausted by his effort.

Wycliffe said, 'What you say is obviously true but it gets us no further. However, while we are here, as part of the routine visits we are making, I would like to see your framing workshop.'

A surprised look; perhaps of relief, 'All right. But I don't know what good it will do.' He gathered himself together and stood up, 'Anyhow, if that is what you want. This way . . . '

They followed him back through the studio and into a room at the far end, a small but seemingly well-equipped workshop. On a central bench there was an elaborate mitring machine. Another bench was laid out with clamps for assembling and gluing, while a third had a device which appeared to be used for the cutting of cardboard mounts. Mouldings of all sorts and sizes were stacked in racks along one wall; and there were cupboards.

'Well, this is it.'

With apparently casual but total irrelevance, Wycliffe asked, 'When did Lina last go to Amsterdam?'

Marsden had deliberately sown the seeds of suspicion about Lina's visits and the pictures she brought back. Whether there was any connection with Francine's death was another matter, but he couldn't afford to neglect the possibility.

Collis was doing a spot of compulsive tidying in the manner of a fussy housewife, and he looked up as though startled by the question. 'Surely you should ask her that.'

'Why? Is it a matter of some secrecy?'

'No . . . No, not at all. It's just that I thought . . . I mean, Lina is Dutch and she visits her relatives in Amsterdam from time to time, as you might expect. Anyway, if it concerns you, she returned from her last visit a week ago last Saturday.'

Lucy Lane asked, 'Had she bought any pictures?'

Hesitation, then, 'Yes. She sometimes buys pictures at auction there. On the whole prices are significantly lower, and when the pound is strong— '

'She sells them on here?'

'Yes, but that is really her business.'

'You mean that it's unconnected with the Guild?'

'That is what I mean. It is a purely private matter.'

Lucy asked, 'Does she bring the pictures back with her?'

'No, they follow as air-freight and they arrive several days later.'

'Are there many as a rule?'

'It varies. Last time there were six, but I really cannot see how this can have any bearing— '

Wycliffe, fencing in the dark, interrupted, 'Do these pictures arrive framed?'

'No – well, yes.' A pause before he added, 'But often unsuitably. As I think I've told you before, we attach a lot of importance to the way a picture is framed.' Collis said this with a finality that was intended to close the subject.

Wycliffe, feeling his way, followed the established principle that those questions which make the witness uncomfortable are most likely to prove worthwhile.

'Do you reframe the ones which need to be?'

'Yes.'

'Would it be possible for us to see any of the pictures which arrived recently?'

Hesitation, then, 'I suppose so but I can't imagine why you would want to.'

'Let's say curiosity; even policemen have their share of that.'

Collis went to a cupboard and lifted out several pictures of differing sizes separated by sheets of bubblewrap, and arranged them in a row against one of the benches.

Collis said, 'All the pictures are removed from their frames on arrival for cleaning. This is a fairly average purchase, nothing spectacular, but readily saleable.' He pointed them out: '*A Café Scene* by Quinsac; a Tom Lloyd, *Rose Garden*; a Robert Henri, *Portrait of a Young Girl*— '

Wycliffe interrupted. 'There are only five; I thought you said six.'

Collis sighed. 'You are playing with me. You know perfectly well that Lina has the sixth picture in her studio for a minor retouch. After all, that was her job, and it is perfectly legitimate.'

'Does Mrs Archer do any original work in her studio?'

'I've no idea. You should ask her.'

Wycliffe decided that without some sort of theory to work on there was little point in pushing Collis further. And he felt pity for the man.

'Very well, Mr Collis. Thank you for your help.'

Outside, Lucy said, 'Does that take us any further?'

'At least we know more about what goes on. Marsden obviously thinks that there's something fishy about Lina's picture-buying and I certainly got that impression talking to Collis. I know nothing about the picture market but I would have thought that making and flogging copies of the sort of thing we've seen would have to be done for love rather than for much in the way of money.'

He broke off. 'Shaw might help us there. Collis is obviously scared but I had the impression that it wasn't so much what we talked about as where the talk might lead. Am I being fanciful?'

'It's one of the privileges of rank, sir. He's like a cat on hot bricks about the whole set-up. He's pathetic. You didn't mention his police record.'

'What would be the point at this stage?'

There is an idea dreamed up by a French mathematician called the 'Cluster Theory', which suggests among other things that even apparently unrelated events occur in clusters.

Odd! But it seems to work in criminal investigation. Either nothing happens, or everything does. Either you are snowed under with fresh information or the case you've built up seems to be falling apart. For days at a time you can be running around in circles trying to cope, or you find yourself thinking that for all the good you are doing you might as well go home.

Perhaps they were in for a spell of the latter.

Statements were being taken from everybody on the site, while a last-resort clip-board team was at work in the village, harvesting gossip. And there was plenty of that. With a hand-picked collection of oddities on your doorstep and a murder, in particular the murder of someone already the subject of local myth and legend, gossip is irresistible.

Wycliffe sat in the van and tried to think constructively; something he found very difficult to do, and which was usually unprofitable.

Francine was dead. She had been murdered in a particularly cold-blooded fashion. These were facts.

There seemed to be several possible lines of inquiry depending on the motive for the killing. Francine had been killed by a frustrated lover. She had been killed because she was a threat to the craft guild of Archer's dream. She had been killed because she knew too much about some major scam involving Lina and others. There was a fourth possibility which had to be considered, that her death was directly linked to her part in the events of ten years ago. The last seemed unlikely though not impossible.

Wycliffe tried to be systematic and consider each in turn but it failed to get him far. The frustrated-lover angle he discarded. Paul was the only real candidate and Paul would not step on the proverbial cockroach let alone harm the girl he had loved, and whose vagaries he had endured for so many years.

To protect the integrity of the Guild?

That pointed only to Archer . . . A fanatic? No doubt. But a murderous fanatic? Just possible, but without some added incentive, some irresistible drive . . .

The picture scam – if it was one? It could be the best bet. Lina's pictures. But it had seemed to him more than once that she was deliberately drawing his attention towards rather than away from her precious pictures.

A link with the past?

He could think of nothing credible unless it concerned Francine's inheritance.

He had his evening meal at the Tributers' with Lucy Lane and afterwards he said, 'You'd better be getting back to the hotel. Get one of the lads to pick you up.'

'What are you doing, if I'm allowed to ask?'

'I've got my bag in the car so I shall stay the night here if Phyllis will have me.'

Phyllis said, 'A room? I've three empty tonight. 'Tis still early in the season for our sort of visitors. Anyway, I'll see your bed is nice an' aired.'

Before bedtime Wycliffe walked down the track towards Mynhager and then followed the footpath out to the point. It was dark, and he could see the flashing beams of Godrevy and Pendeen Watch. The sea was quiet, a vaguely luminous expanse under the stars. And the stars set Wycliffe thinking of other worlds, of boundless space, and endless time. Such thoughts had troubled him as a child, and still did, Einstein and his successors notwithstanding. He hoped that there was a god, at least somebody who might reasonably be expected to know what it was all about. He would feel better if he could believe that.

He walked back to the Tributers'. In the bar Phyllis was cashing up.

She had given him the same room in which he had spent that Christmas night ten years ago, and from a phone in the passage he spoke to Helen and told her so.

'Look after yourself.'

'And you.'

Fifteen minutes of Virginia Woolf's diary put him to sleep.

Chapter Seven

Wednesday

Day four of the inquiry. Wycliffe woke to a sloping ceiling and bare beams, a small square window low down and a grey light. For an instant he was back in the little bedroom of his childhood. A confused night: he seemed to have been dreaming most of the time but he could recall only one dream. Once more he was sitting opposite Archer, across that office desk, and Archer was looking at him, his expression unusually shrewd. 'If only Francine had been a Piscean.'

At breakfast there were two other guests, a middle-aged married couple 'doing' Cornwall in the off season. They had porridge, toast and marmalade; he was given no option but a Phyllis breakfast. Much more of this and he would have to let his belt out a notch.

He drove to the site shortly before nine o'clock. There was patchy sunshine, but once more clouds were closing in from the sea and rain was not far off. In the police van he found Iris Thorne alone, reading through her notes. She had carved out a place for herself in the team as individual and respected as Lucy Lane's. Another very attractive young woman, but as far as Wycliffe knew there was no man in her life. Like Lucy, she lived with her parents and seemed content. There were others like them in the Force and Wycliffe sometimes wondered if these women were inhibited by the job.

'Has DS Wills got anything on Lander?'

'I don't think so, sir. He's been in touch with Exeter CID and they are trying to find somebody who remembers the case.'

Among the papers on the table Wycliffe noticed Francine's two engagement books. 'Any luck with the starred entries?'

Iris frowned. 'I'm not sure how far I've got, sir. Without making too much of an issue of it, I've been using these interviews to find out about the starred dates. One thing seems definite: wherever I've been able to check there is a star against the date on which Lina returned from Amsterdam.'

Iris paused, choosing her words. 'In every case these starred dates are followed by another, six or seven days later and, as far as I've been able to check, these correspond with the arrival of the pictures themselves.'

Wycliffe was pleased. 'So we know that for several months Francine thought it worthwhile to keep a check on Lina's activities. It could lead to something.'

But Iris had not finished. 'There's a complication. For the more recent visits there is yet another starred date, and in each case it's the first Friday following the delivery of the pictures.'

'Any suggestion?'

Iris pouted. 'I haven't a clue. Of course we can't be sure that it has anything to do with the pictures.'

Wycliffe was impressed, and tried to contribute his bit. 'Assuming that it has, I've been told that Lina returned from her last trip to Amsterdam on Saturday May the eighth.'

'Yes, sir. And the pictures were delivered on Friday the fourteenth.'

'So the next starred date should be the following Friday, that's to say the twenty-first – the day after tomorrow.'

Two people pleased with themselves.

'We must keep our eyes and ears open, Iris. Good work!'

The pictures again. Marsden had been disinclined to offer any firm opinion about the pictures except to question them as a major source of income. But Francine must have thought otherwise or the starred entries in her little engagement books would seem to be meaningless.

Lucy Lane arrived and was almost immediately followed by Archer, a distressed Archer. 'I'm sorry to burst in like this but I'm worried. It's my wife . . . I can't understand it!'

He slumped into the chair Wycliffe placed for him. 'She's missing. Her bed hasn't been slept in and I can't find her anywhere . . . ' The large, soft hands were clasped tightly together and the masterful Eric Gill image had altogether disappeared.

'When did you last see her?'

Archer considered. 'Yesterday evening. We had our meal, and by the time we had cleared away it must have been about half-past eight before we went to our rooms to work.' A brief hesitation, then, 'As we have very different sleep patterns we do not share a bedroom, and so we did not meet again last night.'

He stopped speaking and Wycliffe prompted, 'So when did you miss her?'

Archer was having difficulty. 'I must explain that it is often late in the morning before we happen to get together. We have no organised breakfast. This morning I fetched Evadne at eight, as I do every day.' He glanced at his watch. 'It must have been nearly an hour ago, just after nine, that I wanted a word with Lina about something and went in search of her. Evadne said that she hadn't seen her so I went up to her room. As I say, the bed was made up.' A faint smile. 'Lina is Dutch, and airing beds that have been slept in is an article of faith.'

'So what have you done since then?'

Archer shifted on his chair, his hand went to his beard. 'Of course I was concerned. I phoned round but nobody had seen her. There was no reply from Emile's studio so I went along to see for myself. The blinds were drawn and the door was locked. I knocked and called out, but there was no reply. I went back for the spare key but it was missing.'

He looked at Wycliffe and his expression was almost pleading. 'I really can't imagine what can have happened.'

Wycliffe, matter of fact, said, 'Obviously, we must take a look in the studio.'

A few minutes later Wycliffe, Archer and Lucy Lane trooped across to the Archer house, around it and up the slope to Collis's studio. Wycliffe was aware that their procession was probably being watched from every building within range.

Up the steps, and faced with the locked door, Wycliffe performed one of the few tricks he had learned from the best part of a lifetime in association with crime. From his pocket he produced a bit of bent wire and inserted it into the keyhole. A moment or two of delicate fiddling and to his relief and surprise it worked. He opened the door.

The dimly lit studio looked much as he had seen it before: the beach scenes, the veiled portrait of Francine, the painter's litter . . . He led the way towards Collis's living quarters, then stopped. A woman was lying on the floor at his feet, just inside the communicating door.

'Let's have some light!'

He knelt beside the woman. It was Lina Archer. She was lying on her back, her wide-open eyes staring upwards. Her blonde hair was caught back from her face emphasising the strong features. Wycliffe felt for a pulse. There was none, and he realised that rigor was well advanced.

Lina Archer was dead.

The body was fully dressed: a grey woollen jumper, trousers and house shoes. The face was very pale. It was a moment or two before he noticed the cord encircling her neck just below the larynx. It was all but hidden by the high neck of her jumper. Despite the absence of the usual post-mortem symptoms it seemed that Lina had been strangled.

'I am deeply sorry. Your wife is dead.'

Archer let out a muffled cry and turned away.

Wycliffe spoke quietly to Lucy. 'See him back to the house. I'll deal with things here for the moment. Send somebody to hold the fort.'

Without a word Archer allowed himself to be escorted away and Wycliffe was left alone.

From the top of the steps he called Kersey on his mobile. A brief updating, then, 'The whole works, Doug. Get Forbes out here as soon as possible. I'll talk to Franks.'

Franks was his usual self. 'I shall have to get a season ticket. What is it this time? Another monoxide?'

'A woman strangled. At least that's what it seems to me but you may have a different idea.'

Back in the studio he stood looking down at the body and, for the first time, noticed on the floor not far from the head but almost hidden by the open door a sizeable pestle, the sort of thing Collis might have used if he ground his own colours. It could have a story to tell.

Wycliffe entered the living room and went through into the bedroom. Blinds were drawn everywhere and the bed was made up. Otherwise nothing unusual.

Returning, he edged once more past the body and went through the studio to the frame workshop. Nothing much had changed here either, certainly nothing of any relevance to what had happened in the living room.

In more than thirty years as a policeman he could only remember one other occasion when he had been first on the scene of a murder. He would have to give evidence in Court of the discovery: 'At twenty-five minutes past ten on the morning of Wednesday the nineteenth of May last . . . '

An odd situation in which to be rehearsing Court jargon, and a reminder that he was still vulnerable to shock. High time to take himself in hand.

A uniformed constable arrived to stand guard and Wycliffe was released.

It had started to rain, a fine drizzle. Wycliffe walked back to the caravan, both puzzled and troubled.

Two murders: Francine Lemarque and Lina Archer. Presumably by the same hand. Two killers in such a situation defied credulity. In the case of Francine it was possible to envisage a motive, but with this second killing what common motive could there have been?

And Collis was missing.

The troops began to arrive: DI Prisk with DC Curnow in tow and four uniformed men. The Collis premises were taped off. Fox was let loose with Dr Forbes, the police surgeon; neither of them was permitted to disturb anything until Franks had had his say. Forbes would confirm death. Fox would photograph the body *in situ* and everything else.

They were all followed by a pair from Forensic, the plump Florence – 'Don't call me Flo!' – and her assistant. Floodlights were rigged but the blinds remained drawn.

Lucy Lane joined Wycliffe.

Wycliffe asked, 'What's he like?'

'Very shaken but fit to be questioned, I'd say.'

Wycliffe turned to Prisk. 'Let me know when Franks arrives. I shall be in the Archer house. Obviously we'll need statements from everybody concerned, with special attention to those who live on the site.'

Lucy Lane said, 'Archer is in the office with the Penrose woman.'

It was strange to see the man in his office looking, at first sight, as Wycliffe had seen him at the start of the inquiry. Then Lina had joined him; now Evadne Penrose was already at his side.

Archer seemed disorientated and very tired.

Wycliffe was sympathetic. 'I realise that you are in great distress and I would not intrude at this time if it could be avoided but there are questions which must be answered if we are to get the investigation under way.'

Archer nodded. 'I understand.'

'Is it at all likely that your wife might have gone to Collis's studio last night, after you had parted to go to your rooms?'

Archer considered. 'It's certainly possible. Lina has never been one for putting things off. If an idea occurred to her which seemed important and involved Emile, she might well have gone along to discuss it with him.'

'You can make no suggestion as to what the subject might have been this time?'

Archer looked vague. 'I'm afraid not.'

'You realise that Collis is missing?'

A lengthy pause, then, 'Of course I realise he isn't here but I can't believe that he had any part in this terrible thing.'

'I am not suggesting that he had but he must be found.'

Archer stroked his beard. 'The odd thing is that Lina seems to have taken our spare key with her. As I think you know, we have keys to all the site properties but the one to Emile's place is missing.'

'When did you last see Collis?'

Archer frowned. 'I don't remember seeing him at all yesterday but that is not unusual. Indeed, when things are quiet Emile will sometimes go off for a whole day or even overnight. And he's often away at weekends. Of course, he never goes without telling us, but he could have mentioned yesterday's absence to Lina.'

'Do you know where he spends his time when he's away?'

Archer looked blank. 'No, I've no idea.'

'You know of no friends or relatives?'

'No. Emile is a very private man. He doesn't talk about himself and he's not the sort to whom one puts personal questions.'

'Has he taken his car?'

'He always does, and it isn't parked behind the house where he usually keeps it.'

Archer rested his hands on the desk top as though for support and closed his eyes. 'I'm sorry— '

Evadne had not spoken so far but she intervened. 'Can't you see that he's had enough?'

'I won't keep you much longer. What sort of car does Collis drive?'

'A little blue Peugeot 205 diesel.'

'Do you know its registration?'

Archer stirred himself. 'It's an up-country number – K-reg; he bought it second-hand . . . ABO something. I can't get nearer than that.'

Wycliffe stood up. 'I'll leave you for now but we shall talk again and I will keep you informed of any developments.'

Outside, Lucy said, 'Odd!'

'In what way?'

'I don't know. It seemed unreal.'

Wycliffe said, 'It looks bad for Collis. I couldn't make up my mind about him. He's unimpressive but intelligent, a good draughtsman and an adequate painter, able to make a living from his work. But he was scared. Marsden says he was easily led, and he'd had one brush with the law over forged paintings. But murder? Anyway, the sooner we get on his tracks the better, and Lander may be able to help.'

Lucy said, 'I don't trust Lander and it strikes me that there may be more between those two than a gay relationship.'

Wycliffe agreed. 'Well, you've got enough to do a vehicle check and circulate the details. At the same time you must set our people on questioning everybody who spent last night on the site. You don't need me to spell it out.'

He hesitated. 'But before we get down to routine interrogation it might be an idea for us to have a word with one or two of them. I'm sure they know more than they've come up with so far. More perhaps than they think they know, and formal questioning may not be the best way to get at it.'

Lucy Lane said, 'On the same point, I had the impression that Archer was holding something back. I'm not saying that he was lying, just that we didn't get the whole story.'

They were interrupted by a great roar and a slithering of protesting tyres, as Franks' Porsche breasted the grassy slope behind the Archer house and came to a halt outside the Collis building.

Franks got out, followed by Viv, who registered obvious disapproval. He came towards them, rotund and, as ever, pleased with himself.

Wycliffe said, 'Did you have to bring that machine up here?'

Franks looked at Lucy. 'That's the welcome I get! They told me back there that this is where the action is, and I'm not paid to walk.'

In Collis's studio lights blazed and there was a subdued bustle of activity. Dr Forbes presented himself and the two medics went to brood over the body of the victim.

The team from Forensic and Fox, with his assistant, were busy in the living quarters. Fox recorded on film the pathologist's

117

examination of the body while Viv made notes. The Forensic delegation concentrated on a meticulous study of the immediate environment of the crime.

Wycliffe, superfluous, confined himself to the studio and the framing room. It was strange. Within a few feet of the body of a murdered woman, nothing had changed. He brooded on the implications of Archer's account of what must have happened the night before. At some time after going up to her room Lina had apparently left the house, taking with her the spare key of Collis's studio. Had she assumed that Collis would not be there? Or that he would not let her in?

Somebody must have been there, and who else but Collis?

Wycliffe had been wandering aimlessly and came to stand by Collis's portrait of Francine, still hidden behind a cloth. He had been curious about that picture and he removed the cloth. Disappointment. Francine was seated in an armchair, reading. Conventional to the point of boredom. And her face had been painted out. Evidently Collis had experienced difficulty with the face and Wycliffe was not surprised.

At another level he was trying to come to terms with the idea that Collis had murdered Lina Archer by strangulation. It seemed incredible. If only on physical grounds. Lina was a well-built, muscular woman and Collis was close to qualifying as a wimp.

'Dr Franks would like a word, sir.'

Wycliffe followed the constable back to Collis's living room where Lina's body still lay on the floor, though its position had been changed.

'Getting shy of bodies in your old age, Charles? See what our Florence has for us.'

The plump young woman from Forensic was holding a plastic exhibit bag by one corner. It held the pestle he had last seen on the floor near the body. It was about nine inches long with a club-like form.

Franks said, 'There are bloodstains on that thing and a couple of hairs. There is also a nasty wound at the base of the victim's skull.

She was clobbered, Charles, before being strangled. Our killer did a belt and braces job.'

As a weapon, the pestle put a different complexion on Collis's possible guilt.

Franks went on, 'Well, I've done all I can here. They tell me the mortuary boys are on their way so she can be shifted on your say-so. In my opinion, at present, she died of strangulation by means of a nylon cord tightened around her neck below the larynx. But she was already unconscious when that was done.'

'Time of death?'

Franks glanced at his watch. 'It's now half-past one. No lunch again. Anyway, my guess is that she died between ten and midnight.'

Wycliffe walked with Franks to his car. A minute or two later the Porsche slithered down the slope and disappeared around the Archer house, miraculously without mishap.

With Franks gone the studio premises could be handed over to Fox and the people from Forensic. Prisk, with a DC and one of the Forensic team, would accompany the body and attend the post-mortem.

So on physical grounds at least, Collis was back in the running.

Wycliffe was thinking of the Guild of Nine. Two of its members, including the *de facto* chief, had been murdered and another was missing. Archer himself was, presumably, struggling to come to terms with a situation that was both deeply personal and a threat to his whole way of life. He was left with Scawn, the potter, Arthur Gew, Alice Field and a devastated Paul Bateman.

With the whole organisation seeming to fall apart, what were these people thinking, and what did they know?

Time he made contact with his new chief. 'Keep in touch' was the watchword. He telephoned from the police van.

'Your case gets curiouser and curiouser, Charles!' Was it possible that Madam was another disciple of Lewis Carroll? 'You need to keep in with the press in all this. Otherwise we shall have headlines of the "Mass Murderer in Art Colony" genre, and we can do without that.'

It made sense, and Wycliffe spoke to Kersey. 'A press briefing in the morning at your end, Doug. Fix it for eleven.'

Through the window he could see a police refreshment van being manoeuvred into position near the entrance to the site. Murder or no murder, you can't have starving coppers on your hands.

But he still settled for beer and sandwiches at the Tributers'.

Chapter Eight

Wednesday continued

Phyllis's sandwiches with home-cured ham were something to be remembered and should have been followed by a period of rest and meditation but this was unavailable.

Back at the site he found Lucy in the van with Scawn. 'Mr Scawn has news for us.'

Scawn's manner was contrite. 'I'm afraid that Robert has left us. He must have gone at some time during the night.'

'And you've only just got round to telling us?'

Scawn looked uncomfortable. 'I know it looks odd but it's not all that unusual for us not to meet up until the afternoon. This morning I got up late, had a scratch breakfast, then worked in my room on a couple of new designs that I have in mind. I assumed that Robert was in the pottery, sorting out the stuff unloaded from the kiln yesterday.'

Scawn paused and drew a deep breath before continuing. 'At some time after two I went down to take a look. Robert wasn't there, and nothing had been done. To cut my story short I discovered that his motorcycle was missing and, when I went to his room, it was obvious that he had gone off with the more portable of his belongings.'

'But you hadn't heard him drive off?'

'No, but it's quite possible for him to freewheel down to the road if he chooses. He does that when it suits him.'

'So you've no idea at all when he left.'

Scawn was regretful. 'I'm afraid not. And I have to say that I am astonished and disappointed by his behaviour.'

Wycliffe was official. 'Thank you, Mr Scawn. That will be all for the present, but you will be asked to make a formal statement for the record.'

Scawn stood up, looked vaguely about him, and left.

Lucy said, 'Turmoil in the flux. Anyway, we'd better circulate Lander and his bike.'

'Has anything more come through on him?'

'Nothing specific. Dave Wills has been in touch with Exeter and they're trying to locate Lander's family, although the whole story that he fed to Scawn could be on a par with his alleged relationship.'

'I suppose it's possible that he and Collis have gone off together.'

Lucy said, 'The thought occurred to me. We shall soon have nobody left.'

'No news of Collis? Or of his car?'

'Nothing so far, sir.'

'We're getting nowhere fast, Lucy.'

'You don't feel that we might be on the last lap?'

Wycliffe was mildly derisive. 'Collis murdered Francine by blocking the flue of her bath heater, now he's strangled Lina and cleared out, running scared. Is that what you think?'

Lucy was equal to that. 'I suppose you intended that as irony, but what you're saying sounds credible to me.' She hesitated, then, 'You saw the blocking of that flue as a woman's trick, and though I didn't agree I understood what you were getting at. Times are changing but I believe that most women intent on murder will, understandably, still avoid the direct physical violence that comes more easily to a man.'

Wycliffe finished for her. 'And Collis, though an accredited male, is sexually ambivalent. You may have a point, Lucy, but it doesn't appeal to me. In any case, can you see Collis strangling Lina? Even allowing for the pestle, I would find it more credible the other way round.'

Lucy pondered. 'I'm not so sure. Collis is slight of build but I don't see him as a weakling. And she could have driven him too far over the picture business; he's been depressed and worried for some time, and now that we know his background and his record— '

Wycliffe said, 'This picture business seems to be the chorus of every verse. Anyway, changing the subject, have you heard anything from Fox?'

'No, he's still at the studio and so is the Forensic team.'

'Then let's hear what they have to say for themselves.'

The lights were still on in the Collis building. They found Fox with his assistant at work in the living quarters. The Forensic team was packing up, and the white-coated Florence reported: 'I've finished here. The deceased's clothing and certain specimens will be taken for laboratory examination.' Florence's earnest blue eyes seemed to question whether Wycliffe's understanding was up to this statement of technical procedures. 'Anyway, you will have my report on Friday morning.'

'I shall look forward to it.'

Wycliffe turned to Fox. 'Anything?'

Fox was subdued. 'Nothing of obvious significance, sir. I'm puzzled.'

Fox admitting to being puzzled; a first, as far as Wycliffe could remember.

Fox enlarged. 'I'm struck by the absence of anything really personal. I mean, there were no letters, no bills, no bank statements and no documents of any sort – no passport, birth certificate or driving licence . . . And no photographs.'

'Do you get the impression that these things have been recently removed? Or that he didn't in the ordinary way keep them here?'

In his time Fox had delved into the lives of a great many people as seen through their cupboards, closets and drawers. So he spoke with authority.

'My guess is that he saw himself as lodging, rather than living here, sir. I suspect he had a base somewhere else.'

Wycliffe was impressed. If Collis had a hideaway it would explain his mysterious absences, perhaps including the present one. 'So what did you actually find?'

'Here in the flat, apart from his everyday needs, there's very little. There are quite a few books on the history of art, several paperback novels, a few magazines and a newspaper or two. Not much else, other than the tools of his trade.'

Wycliffe was beginning to feel more kindly disposed towards Fox. And Fox was not through.

'Prints taken from Collis's living quarters suggest that he had a regular male visitor and that they were on intimate terms. The prints occur in the sitting room, kitchen, bathroom and bedroom. Some are quite recent.'

Wycliffe said, 'Almost certainly Lander. I'd like you to check on Lander's room and see if there's a match. And anything else you can find there, especially anything that might give a clue to his background.'

At four o'clock, back in the caravan, news of a development came through from the Incident Room. A patrol car covering neighbouring cliff and moorland roads and tracks as part of the 'no stone unturned' routine had found Collis's car, abandoned.

Lucy took down details, including the map reference. 'Do you want to go there?'

She spread a map on the table. 'Here it is.' Her pencil indicated a point on the road which crossed the moor, linking the coast road in the north with Penzance in the south. The whole distance was no more than six miles as time-conscious crows are said to fly. A little longer, taking into account the vagaries of the terrain.

Lucy went on, 'It's just beyond New Mill, less than three miles from the outskirts of Penzance.'

Wycliffe knew that road well enough – they used it for their trips to and from Penzance. In a drive lasting less than fifteen minutes the rugged cliffs and barren moors of the north were exchanged for a low-lying coast, a magnificent bay and the rich soil of the south.

Lucy said, 'According to the report the car was found early this morning, parked just off the road in a field gateway.'

Wycliffe was puzzled. 'What was he up to? He must have driven there, ditched his car and just cleared off. But where?'

'Do you want me to lay on a team for collection and assessment?'

'We'll see for ourselves first.'

They drove up on to the moor and along the unfenced track across land rich in pickings for the archaeologist but offering little or nothing to the modern farmer. Wycliffe wondered why the Iron Age people apparently chose to work this unrewarding terrain. Probably they were more concerned with pasture than cultivation. There followed a pattern of tiny fields and then the road dipped down into a valley with trees, leading into the odd little village of New Mill which, to Wycliffe, looked as though it ought to be an appendage of some stately home, but wasn't.

Just beyond the village they came upon a patrol car sheltering a uniformed PC, presumably guarding the blue Peugeot 205 parked ahead of him. The little car was several yards from the nearest field entrance.

The PC shifted himself and joined them. 'Constable Jago, sir. The farmer moved it first thing this morning when he wanted to get his tractor into the field. I haven't touched it.'

Wycliffe recognised the breed. They make a cult of doing nothing about anything in case there's any blame about.

Jago went on, 'Apparently the car was unlocked, with the key in the ignition and the farmer tried to drive it, but though it started, it died on him. The tank was empty, so he just pushed it out of his way to where it is now.'

'When did he first see the car?'

'This morning. It must have been left there at some time during the night. He assumed that it belonged to some guy, well over the limit, who would come back and collect it after he'd sobered up.'

Wycliffe muttered, 'It makes no sense but where was he going?'

Lucy offered, 'Penzance station to catch a train?'

'If he was making a getaway, why draw attention to himself by catching a train when he had a car? . . . No, don't tell me! It's possible that Lander picked him up on his pillion and they went off together.'

Lucy was becoming impatient. 'In which case they could be

anywhere by now. But isn't it about time we attended to the routine?'

'What? Yes, of course. Arrange for the Vehicle Examiners to take a look, then remove it to their garage and hand over to Forensic.' After a pause, he added, 'Though what we can expect them to tell us, I can't imagine.'

He had in his mind an absurd picture of Collis, lumbered with a couple of suitcases, tramping through the darkness and the rain. 'The Runaway' – a black and white illustration from a Victorian novel.

'Presumably Collis has been listed as missing?'

'Of course.'

'Then get a couple of chaps on a house-to-house in the village and along the road from the coast. This isn't the M25 and those little diesel Peugeots make themselves heard.'

'But if somebody did see the car drive past in the middle of the night, what good would that do us?'

'None, but we might turn up something.' Wycliffe looked at the dismal dripping hedgerow and the narrow ribbon of tarmac snaking away into the mist and said, 'Anyway there's nothing more here for us. Let's get back to the caravan. At least we can have a coffee.'

In the car Lucy was silent and Wycliffe said, 'Lost your tongue?'

'No, I'm just wondering if it's safe to use it.'

Wycliffe said, 'On the face of it Collis is a fugitive, wanted for questioning in connection with two murders. That's the scenario to which we have to respond.'

'But you've got reservations?'

'Haven't you? Anyway he's got to be found. Somebody must know where he spent those times when he was away from the site. After all, Fox is an experienced man and by no means the fool he pretends to be. He thinks Collis had another place – a hideaway if you like, and everything points to that.'

They arrived back on the site. 'Let's break the news to Archer, I want to see how he reacts.'

The office was empty but the ubiquitous Evadne arrived. 'He's been lying down but he's up now. I'll tell him you're here.'

There was no need. Archer joined them, looking flushed and on edge. 'You've got news of Emile?'

Wycliffe told him.

Archer shook his head. 'I can't understand it! I mean, why would he do this to Lina? They were close . . . It's beyond me . . . ' A ghost of a smile. 'And he'd run out of diesel. That's Emile! It's not the first time . . . Near New Mill, you say . . . But where was he going? And where is he now?'

'We've no idea but we have to find him. You can make no suggestion?'

Archer frowned. 'I wish I could.'

'Does he have a mobile phone?'

'Yes, he does and I think he kept it in his car.'

'So, when he ran out of diesel he could have phoned someone to come and pick him up.'

'I suppose so, but I've no idea who.'

And that was that.

Outside, Lucy asked, 'A grieving husband?'

Wycliffe did not answer and they took refuge in the caravan, empty at the moment, but now available to the whole team and cared for by nobody. File copies of statements sent over from the Incident Room littered the table along with plastic coffee cups, and cigarette ash, and squeezed-up balls of discarded paper.

Wycliffe let his temper show. 'This place is a shambles, Lucy! Tell somebody to clean it up, and all of them to keep it that way.'

Lucy tidied superficially while Wycliffe got coffee out of the machine, and they sat down. The mist had closed in and their outlook was circumscribed. The silence was absolute, punctuated only by the plaintive bleat of the foghorn at Godrevy. Presumably the work of the Guild was going on in those invisible little buildings close by, but in the caravan there was a sense of total isolation and so it seemed that whatever was done or said it could have no real significance.

Wycliffe cleared his throat and tried to clear his mind. 'The truth is, Lucy, that we are skirting around the crucial question of motive. Why was Francine murdered? Why Lina?'

'Good questions,' from Lucy, drily.

'If we take Francine first, the most plausible answer so far seems to be that Francine knew, or guessed, that there was something fishy going on in the Guild.'

Wycliffe picked up his plastic coffee mug, discovered it was empty, replaced it on the table and tried again. 'Now, from Iris Thorne's work on the starred diary entries it looks as though there was some fraud concerning Lina and her imported pictures. There are indications that Collis was involved, probably in copying or faking of some sort – work for which he has experience and talent.'

Lucy nodded. 'So the girl tried to use her knowledge against the pair of them and paid the penalty. I suppose it hangs together as a motive for her murder.'

Wycliffe shifted uncomfortably on his bench. 'Until it falls apart. There's a snag. Marsden is sure that with what is known of the value and status of Lina's pictures it could be no more than a small-scale fiddle. In fact, he wonders why she bothered unless she did it for kicks. If Marsden is right, and he should know, it doesn't look like the kind of scam that might lead to murder. And Lina – why would Collis kill her?'

'All right. So where do we go from here?' Lucy with mild irritation. 'Can there be anything in the sex angle? Variations on the theme of a frustrated lover?'

'But who are the possible candidates? We've already dismissed Collis from that role and we don't see Paul Bateman as a killer. Of course there's Blond Bob about whom we know little enough. We can't afford to ignore any possibility, but on present showing I don't think we shall get far down that road. And even if we have a feasible motive for Francine's murder it doesn't apply to Lina.'

Lucy was silent and Wycliffe went on, 'There is another possibility that occurs to me, though in some ways it sounds even less credible than the others: Francine's money. But as I've said before there's much more to this than money, Francine's or anybody else's.'

'You're thinking of Archer?'

'Who else? The idea occurred to Scawn but only, I think, as a sick joke.'

'And Lina? It doesn't explain what happened to her.'

'Are we dealing with two killers?'

'It's just not credible.'

That evening Lucy returned to Penzance while Wycliffe decided on another night at the Tributers'. News of the second murder did not make early evening radio or TV news so he was allowed to have his meal in peace.

Mackerel fillets in an egg, butter and herb sauce. Cornish to her toenails, Phyllis was not above filching from Elizabeth David. But who is?

Afterwards he walked to Gurnard's Head. High cloud obscured the sky and reached to just above the horizon. But as he watched, an angry sun emerged below the cloud and sank slowly into Homer's wine-dark sea.

There was no living thing in sight, and not a single human artefact, but Wycliffe did not feel alone; just part of the theatre.

He walked back to The Tributers' and had a drink at the bar, feeling that he was returning from an excursion into a different world.

Early to bed.

But before that he made his phone call to Helen.

Helen said, 'I had a call from Ruth this evening. She's moving to a new job with an advertising agency in Baker Street. She's on top of the world.'

'I'm glad, but I wish she would marry and settle down.'

Helen laughed. 'That's always been my line until now. Anyway, sleep well.'

'And you.'

Chapter Nine

Thursday

Wycliffe had one of those dreamless sleeps which are denied to us by psychiatrists who, apparently, sacrifice long nights to the study of eye movements in their sleeping subjects. However, the illusion was enough for him to awake refreshed. A shower. Phyllis had modernised the essentials, leaving the fabric of the building and the decor to rusticity. Wycliffe's breakfast was all but spoiled by the eight o'clock news.

'We are receiving reports of a second murder at the Cornish craft centre, where the body of a young woman was found on Sunday morning. The police have so far released no details of this second death but they are treating it as murder. The victim is believed to be a woman in her late forties, a leading figure in the affairs of the craft centre. The police have already been investigating possible links with a tragedy in the same area ten years ago when three people, including Gerald Bateman, a well-known political figure of the time, died by violence . . . '

Wycliffe left his toast and marmalade untouched.

From his car he spoke to Kersey. 'All set for blast-off at eleven? I think we are in for a rough passage . . . Yes, I shall be there on time.'

Once more the team would be questioning everybody on the site concerning what they might have seen or heard, but also and in greater detail about relationships, tensions and suspicions, real or imagined.

Wycliffe felt protective about Paul and decided to tackle him himself.

He drove to the site. The mist had cleared and it was a fine morning. He walked across to the wood-carving shop but the door was locked.

Arthur Gew saw him. 'The boy hasn't been in since Monday. Poor lad. He's really knocked up. All because of a woman. And now we've lost our leader. What next, I ask?' But Gew showed no signs of distress.

Wycliffe joined Lucy Lane in the caravan.

'No sign of the missing Bob, sir. He's no record – not as Lander, anyway. Of course, it's quite possible that he's nothing to do with our business but if his past is at all dicey he could have cleared out on the principle that you don't hang about where there's trouble.

'Scawn seems upset about the whole affair but either because he can't be or won't be, he's not much help. He did, under a bit of pressure, come up with a snapshot of him with Lander at the entrance to the pottery. It's not very good but I've sent it to the lab to see what they can do with it.'

Kersey was right. Delegation works.

'Anything else?'

'Just that Exeter CID are going through the voters' lists for the whole area in search of Landers. Nothing yet. So his whole story seems to have been phoney.'

Lucy turned the pages of her notes. 'And that's about it, sir.'

Wycliffe was pleased but refrained from saying so. There was a tacit assumption of competence between them so that compliments were apt to sound patronising.

'I want a word with young Paul. He's not on the site so I'm going to Mynhager.'

The harsh rugged lines of Mynhager stood out like an etching against the brilliant background of sea and sky. The courtyard was dank and gloomy; the bell shattered a silence that was total.

'Oh, Charles!'

It would take more than murder to change Caroline's ritual responses. But the 'do come in' which followed was less assured and he guessed that his arrival was inopportune.

'You know us well enough by now, Charles . . . We can't treat you like a stranger.'

He was taken into the kitchen where the table held the remains of breakfast.

Virginia had her newspaper spread amid the debris, working on the crossword, cigarette in hand, a saucer for an ashtray. 'For God's sake, Carrie, haven't we got a drawing room?' She glanced across the table at the stained cloth, at the random assemblage of china and at her own contribution. 'Well, there's not much point now.'

Caroline said, 'Has something happened?'

'You haven't heard?'

He told them.

'You're saying she was murdered?'

'Yes.'

Caroline paused in the middle of clearing the table. 'I always said there was something wrong with that place. I didn't like Paul going there. And now— '

'Is Paul about? I would like a word – I shan't upset him.'

'He's up in his room. He's had scarcely any breakfast. He's not eating enough to feed a cat. You know his room, it's across from the one that used to be Father's.'

Up three flights of stairs, the last narrow and twisted. A tiny landing with a window like an arrow slit. He was in the tower. He remembered 'Father's' room but resisted the temptation to look inside to see if it had changed. Almost certainly it had not been disturbed since the old man's death. The sisters were not innovators.

He knocked on the other door and got a 'come in!'

The room was the size of a large cupboard but flooded with light from a window that looked out to sea and down the coast in a vast panorama.

Wycliffe said, 'I suppose you get used to it.'

'Yes.' Paul had been sitting at a draughtsman's table working on a design, presumably for a carving. There was room for that and a bed, but little else.

Paul was very pale but seemingly composed.

'I want to talk to you about Lina.'

'I heard about it this morning.' He glanced at a little radio perched, with several books, on a shelf by the bed.

'You realise this puts what happened to Francine in a different light.'

'I see that.'

'I must tell you two things that were not mentioned in the radio report. Both Emile and Robert Lander are missing. They were neither of them seen after some time on Tuesday. Collis's car has been found abandoned and out of fuel just beyond New Mill. We have nothing on Lander or his motorcycle.'

Paul said, 'I don't understand it.'

'No, but you may be able to help us with background. I want to know, and you want to know, who is responsible for what has happened.'

A moment for reflection, then, 'Yes. Of course! I'll do anything I can.'

'You must have talked to Francine about things that went on in the Guild about which there was gossip. In her little engagement book she starred certain days which seem to correspond with Lina's visits to Amsterdam – the day she left, the day she returned, the day the pictures arrived . . . Did she ever mention any of this to you?'

He looked puzzled. 'Never. She knew that I worried about her . . . ' He hesitated. 'That I thought she would only stir up trouble by enquiring into things which didn't really concern us.'

'Did she ever say anything in particular about Lander or Collis?'

More hesitation. 'Bob Lander was something of a mystery to everybody. It was generally accepted that Lina only tolerated him because of Derek Scawn.'

'So?'

'Well, Fran said that was only a sham, that she was sure Bob and Lina were involved in something and she was determined to find out what.'

'And Emile?'

Paul considered. 'Fran seemed to think he was doing work for Lina that was nothing to do with the Guild.'

'What sort of work?'

'I don't know.'

'Could it have been copying pictures?'

He frowned. 'Possibly. At one time Fran mentioned something about framing but it didn't seem to make sense to me. I mean, we all knew that Emile did the framing but he told Fran something about framing in the Oude Kerk in Amsterdam. I know no more than that.'

Wycliffe had to be content.

Half an hour later he was facing a dozen press persons and a couple of TV cameras in the Incident Room at Penzance.

'Do you connect the murder of Francine Lemarque with her part in the death of her father, Gerald Bateman, the politician, ten years ago?' Ponderous question, but it got in most of the potentially spicy elements.

'I have no reason to suspect that there is any causal connection.'

'Is it likely that her death was linked to the substantial legacy she received shortly before she died?'

'That is one line of investigation but so far we have no evidence to support the idea.'

'Presumably you are treating her death and that of Lina Archer as connected?'

'It would be remarkable if they were not.'

'Will you comment on rumours concerning fraudulent activity within this Guild of Nine?'

'I have no evidence to support any such rumours at the moment.'

Then, from a wag, 'Have you considered consulting the stars?'

'We do not have an astrologer on our team at present.'

'Is it the case that two important witnesses are missing?'

'We are anxious to get in touch with Robert Lander, an assistant in the pottery department, and with Emile Collis, the Guild's painter. Mr Collis's car, a blue Peugeot 205, was found abandoned on the Penzance side of the village of New Mill, on Wednesday.'

And so on . . . And so on . . . Wycliffe was too old-fashioned to welcome press inquisitions, or even to look as though he did. His policy for the most part was to stonewall, but long association had bred a mutual tolerance which usually allowed him to get away with it.

At any rate, it was over at last.

When he was about to return to the site DS Shaw arrived to report on his investigations into Francine's inheritance, the financial background of the Guild, and anything else where there was a smell of money.

Wycliffe had long recognised the value of Shaw's links with those – for him – closed worlds of money and information technology, so Shaw had been encouraged to operate on a long leash.

'The girl's inheritance first. As soon as she heard about the money she went to a lawyer – Hicks and Bone in St Ives. Bone, the surviving partner, is a wily old bird and he was fascinated by the girl. Francine had firm ideas about what she intended to do, and all she asked of him was advice about how to do it.'

Shaw put on his glasses and consulted his notes. 'Her legacy amounted to something over eighty-five thousand pounds, of which she intended to invest fifty in the Guild if she could come to terms with the Archers.'

Shaw broke off. 'Bone tried to talk her into getting financial advice but she got up to walk out, so he held his peace. Then, at the same session, she insisted on him drafting her will.'

Shaw looked at Wycliffe. 'You're going to like this, sir. The whole of her estate is bequeathed to Paul Bateman, with the exception of five thousand pounds which goes to Hugh Marsden, if he survives her.'

'And that will stands?'

'Completed and witnessed according to Bone.'

Shaw continued. 'Anyway, now we come to the Guild's finances. They are a private company and they seem to conform with their articles. Archer keeps his gallery accounts, and Lina her picture accounts, quite separate. The Guild makes a decent profit, Archer's venture pays its way and Lina's picture dealing is in credit, though it hardly seems worth the trouble.

'Anyway, Archer made no difficulty about giving me access and he was helpful in persuading the bank to co-operate without a lot of legal flannel.'

'So, no evidence of any major scam?'

'Not that I can find. If there is any funny business going on – and there may be – it's well covered up.'

Wycliffe sat in his little office off the Incident Room. Marsden, a beneficiary under Francine's will. Talk about twists of fate! And Paul Bateman, a well-off young man.

Should it affect his approach to the case? He dismissed the idea.

As to the rest of Shaw's report, any suggestion of a major scam remained a matter for speculation.

The routine work was going ahead: statements were being fed into the computer; reports were coming in; officers were still out on the ground. But Wycliffe realised that without some new development they were unlikely to get very far.

He leafed through preliminary faxes from the Vehicle Examiner and from Forensic. Next to nothing nicely wrapped up in jargon. The report on Collis's car was a masterpiece. It showed conclusively that anyone *could* have driven the car but that there was no evidence that anyone other than Collis did.

Franks' report on the Lina Archer autopsy had arrived. It stretched the six sentences over the telephone to three pages of close type. Fine for the lawyers, but for Wycliffe, one sentence was enough: 'Lina Archer was rendered unconscious by a blow to the occiput before being strangled.'

Wycliffe skimmed it all. Just in case.

Then lunch with Kersey, and afterwards back to the site. It seemed that he could have conducted his case just as well from a chair in his office and earned Brownie points, but away from the action (not that there was much) he felt lost.

He joined Lucy in the police caravan and, together, they went in search of Scawn. They found him in the pottery, apparently at a loose end and surprisingly apprehensive.

'You want to talk to me? But there's nothing I can tell you that you don't know already.'

They followed him upstairs and when they were settled, Wycliffe said, 'Since we last talked the situation has changed radically.'

'You mean that Lina has been murdered. I am shocked, I simply do not know what to think and—'

Wycliffe cut him short. 'Lina has been murdered and Lander and Collis have both disappeared. As far as Lander is concerned, although well aware of his capacity for fantasy, you apparently accepted without question the account he gave you of his immediate family and of his visits to them.'

A rueful smile, 'I have to admit that I was taken in. His stories concerning his parents, and their problems, were so circumstantial that they seemed in a quite different category from, for example, his tale about our alleged relationship.' A pause, 'Of course, it was not I who employed him in the first place, but Lina, so I had no access to any correspondence there may have been.'

One of the Siamese cats jumped on to Scawn's knees, flexing its claws before settling down. It must have been painful, but Scawn gave no sign.

Wycliffe's manner was official. 'I am going to ask you a question, Mr Scawn, to which I want a clear, unequivocal answer. Have you at any time suspected that Lander was involved in some illicit activity here – perhaps something which involved Collis and Lina?'

The brown eyes showed concern. 'Unequivocal, you say. It is difficult to be at all specific. As I've told you, I've always found Robert a pleasant person to have about the place, helpful, intelligent, quick to learn and anxious to be agreeable.'

'But?'

Scawn frowned. 'Robert likes to be mysterious – to pretend that he is privy to all sorts of secrets about which his lips are sealed.' A faint smile. 'I don't take him too seriously. It seems to be a somewhat childish aspect of his character and I find it amusing.'

'Can you give examples of the kind of thing?'

Scawn considered. 'He makes remarks like, "You don't know the half of what goes on in this place," or, "Lina is a very clever woman. If Archer only realised . . ." '

'Has he ever mentioned Lina's trips to Amsterdam and the pictures she bought there?'

Very gently, Scawn lifted the cat from his lap on to the floor before replying, 'Yes, he has. Lina's visits and her pictures were becoming a subject of gossip on the site anyway, stirred up, I believe, by Francine.'

'Has Lander ever implied that there was something dubious about Lina's transactions?'

A moment for reflection, then, 'Oh, I think so – yes. But as with all Robert's remarks of that kind, his manner conveys more than his words. I am really out of my depth in all this, Mr Wycliffe.'

Wycliffe seemed to accept this and Lucy Lane took his silence to be her cue. 'Can you tell us anything about the relationship between Lander and Collis?'

It required a moment or two for Scawn to adjust. 'It's clear that Robert has a problem with women, but he went out of his way to be agreeable to Francine. On the other hand Collis and he are certainly close.'

Lucy lost patience. 'Do you think they are having a gay relationship?'

Scawn gave up. 'I think that is very likely but that sort of thing doesn't bother me.'

Lucy said, 'All part of the flux.'

Scawn, on the point of a too-hasty rejoinder, changed his mind. 'I suppose so.'

Wycliffe felt that they had got as far as they were likely to and stood up. 'Well, thank you Mr Scawn. No doubt we shall be back.'

It was one of those dead afternoons with no worthwhile 'input' but at least he was learning to think in terms of the new vocabulary.

That evening he had a leisurely meal with Kersey and Lucy Lane in the hotel dining room. Afterwards he felt in need of one of his walks but, too tired, he settled for a meandering stroll along the promenade.

The mist had cleared and over the sea the stars were coming out. It was almost dark.

The Mount, the Lizard light, the gleaming, rippling sea – they were all putting on their show but he was unappreciative.

Two murders, two witnesses missing, and no obvious way ahead . . .

Recently, as he sometimes did, he had dipped into Ronald Clark's *Freud*. 'Dipped' was the word; he found larger helpings of Freud indigestible and he had some sympathy with the lady who said, 'If that man is right, then we are none of us very nice.'

It was word association which had caught his attention in this latest dip. Once upon a time it had been tried as a tactic in police work and off and on for the past two or three days he had been trying it out on himself. He did so now: sea – ships – sailors – Nelson – Trafalgar Square – The National Gallery – pictures . . .

He had startled himself. Did it really work? Or had his subconscious led him to the subject of his latest preoccupation? But that could be the point anyway . . .

He tried again: pictures – Collis – frame shop – frames – Paul Bateman – Francine – Mynhager . . .

Frames – Paul Bateman? He must have gone astray. Odd! What had Paul to do with pictures? – or with frames? It hadn't worked. Never mind; it was only a silly private game he'd been playing.

But as he walked back to the hotel he was made uncomfortable by the feeling that he had missed something.

He was late with his phone call to Helen. 'I've been wool-gathering.'

'I suppose it's as good an excuse as any other. Sleep tight.'

It was two-fifteen by his little bedside clock when he woke. It often happened that after his first sleep he would lie awake for half an hour, running over in his mind the events of the day. Memories would come back to him in pictures, like shots on a television screen; and in phrases which he seemed to hear in the voice that had spoken them. His problem, or so he believed, was an inability to fit all this into a pattern – to be *logical*.

He could see Paul's room at Mynhager, that little cell, open to the great plain of the sea.

He was trying to get the young man to talk, to unwind a little. Paul was regretting Francine's attempts to probe into Lina's supposedly dubious activities which, she believed, involved Emile.

Perhaps she had proof that he was copying pictures to be sold as originals? Wycliffe still wondered. Though, so far, in following that line he had come up against the snag that there could be no real money in it, certainly not the price of murder.

And Paul, pensive and slow, had said that at one time Francine had mentioned something about framing – whether Collis framed them, or whether it was done in the Oude Kerk in Amsterdam.

Pictures – Collis – frame shop – frames – Paul Bateman . . . It had worked, after all. But did it mean anything? 'I shall have to think about it.'

He turned over. 'But not now.'

Chapter Ten

Friday

Breakfast at the hotel, the short walk to the Incident Room, a mini briefing, another phone conversation with his deputy at head-quarters and, by shortly before ten, he was driving out of Penzance on his way to the Guild site.

A clear day with a great expanse of intensely blue sky, but there was a bank of mist on the horizon. Outlook unsettled. But who wants settled weather? Those who do should avoid Cornwall where each day is an adventure, and weather forecasters pretend not to notice.

The sixth day of the inquiry. Some murder inquiries stretch over months, even years; for some the file is never closed. But these are usually 'open' cases with an undefined range of possible suspects, and no clear indication of rational motive. Here Wycliffe was dealing with murder in a small, almost a closed, community; the range of suspects and of motive were both limited, and the locality was defined.

Arriving at the Guild site he deliberately avoided being seen from the police van and, feeling guilty, he wandered around without an idea in his head. He consoled himself with the words of his DI, when he was still a DS: 'You think too much, Charlie. Keep your ears and your eyes open. Remember the three Ls: Look, Listen and Learn.'

He was vaguely depressed. Often cases reached a stalemate with nothing happening to open up fresh lines of investigation. In this instance too much was happening too quickly: a second murder and the disappearance of two, perhaps crucial, witnesses. He muttered to himself unprofitably, 'Collis and Lander *must* be found!' A house-to-house was under way over a wide area; staff at Penzance Station had been interviewed, and taxi and hire-car drivers questioned, all without result.

His wanderings had taken him to the west side of the stream, past the Guild-hall, and near to the group of buildings that housed the pottery, the wood-carvers' shop and Arthur Gew's whatever. Gew's place was nearest and the door was open so he went in.

He found himself in a smallish room with a bench and walls lined with shelves, pigeon holes and drawers, all bearing labels. Every inch of space seemed to be utilised.

'What do you want? I'm in here.'

Wycliffe went through. Another small room with a bench, a tiny kiln, a row of glass jars containing brightly coloured powders, a minute vice . . .

'Oh! So Muhammad has come to the mountain.'

'Detective Superintendent Wycliffe.'

'I know who you are, but I wondered if I rated a visit. This is my enamelling shop. Your girl probably told you that I'm the jack-of-all-trades in this establishment. She may not have added that I'm master of all of 'em.'

The little man was perched on a stool by the bench, heels caught on the crossbar. 'I'm tidying up. Can't find the will to do much else.' He added after a pause, 'This place is finished.'

'You think so?'

Gew looked at Wycliffe with his tiny brown eyes, serious as a child's. 'I know so, mister. Without our Lina to drum up business and keep Archer in line we shall find ourselves running around in nightshirts with our birth signs stencilled on our bottoms – and damn-all to do. Those of us who stay, that is.'

'Will you be one of them?'

'Oh, yes. Whatever my birth sign, I was born to be on any sinking ship that happens to be around.'

'So you were an admirer of Lina?'

Gew considered. 'That would be pushing it. I admired her drive.

She was our meal chit. But as a woman . . . I'm old-fashioned where women are concerned. But don't ask me what that means. Anyway, if you've come to talk you'd better bring up a stool.'

Wycliffe did, and decided to try his luck at striking a productive chord. 'Francine and Lina have been murdered; Collis and Lander are missing. Any comments?'

An appreciative look. 'So it's gloves off! That suits me. You mentioned Collis. Collis was supposed to be Lina's lap-dog – hers to command. So he was, but he didn't like the role one little bit, and recently he's been trying to get out from under. She had some hold over him and she was using him, but for what purpose I have never discovered. Picture faking comes to mind but I've a feeling there was more to it than that.'

'You seem surprisingly well informed.'

Gew turned on his stool. 'Isn't that what you want?'

'I'm simply wondering how you manage it.'

Gew smiled. 'I live here alone, I've no friends or relations and no real interest outside my work, so I devote myself to knowing other people's business and it suits me. It's less physically demanding than golf or bowls, and a hell of a lot less boring than fishing.'

'Do you have any view on Lander's relationship with Lina?'

Gew picked up a tiny pair of tweezers from his tray of little tools and began to play with it. 'Oh, Bob Lander simply did what he was told by Madam.' A mischievous smile. 'But I thought the great detective might have been more interested in the relationship between Madam and Lander's boss.'

Wycliffe waited.

Gew was enjoying himself. 'I said nothing of this while Madam was still with us, but now . . . Well, things have changed. You may not know that she was a more or less regular visitor at the pottery. Of course, those visits could have been on matters of business but, if so, they took place at odd times. Usually, it seems, in what we call the small hours.'

'You mean that she visited Scawn at night? Were these visits frequent?'

A dismissive gesture. 'I've never kept regular watch, Mr

Wycliffe! . . . It's simply that I don't sleep well and I sometimes find myself looking out of the window when I should be in bed. All I can say is that several times during the past year I've seen Madam on her way to or from the pottery during the night or in the early morning.'

'I suppose you have no idea whether Archer was aware of this?'

Gew was ironic. 'Now I come to think of it, I've never asked him.'

Wycliffe, feeling that he had not shone in this interview, but satisfied that there was no more to come, got off his stool. 'Well, thank you, Mr Gew. You've been most helpful.'

Gew did not see his visitor off. He said, 'I've made myself an expert in other people's business, Mr Wycliffe. I may well do a Ph.D. in it when one of our sociologically minded universities gets round to the idea.'

Outside, that bank of mist had moved in, moist and all-pervading. Oblivious, Wycliffe trudged across the site. Lina and Scawn. The mind boggled, but sex can be a great facilitator. It's living together that brings out the problems.

However, the question remained: did Archer know?

Wycliffe passed the Archer house and continued up the slope to Collis's studio. He was making for the framing shop. At the back of his mind he was still brooding on the word association game which had recalled Paul Bateman's reference to Francine's mention of framing at some place in the Oude Kerk.

Arriving at the top of the steps, he broke the police seal and went in.

On the face of it nothing had changed since his first visit five days before. The two embryonic beach scenes were still on their easels and the drape over the third easel still, presumably, concealed Collis's attempt to capture Francine on canvas. Now Francine was dead, Lina was dead. And Collis . . . ?

Wycliffe made for the framing shop.

There were several cupboards and he opened each one. He found the unframed pictures which Collis had shown him, the fruits of Lina's last visit to Amsterdam. Nothing to add to his suspicions there. In other cupboards there were ready-made frames sorted according to size and design – just what one might expect in a frame shop.

But it was in one of these cupboards that he discovered an oddity – a type of frame quite different from any of the others. There were six of them, identical with each other, and he removed one to examine it in detail. The frame was very light, made of a pale grey plastic material. In section and proportion the moulding was little different from some of the wooden frames. Wycliffe was about to put it back when he noticed that there was a small ridge in the plastic, midway along each side of the frame. He examined the ridges more closely and realised that the frame seemed to consist of four right-angled 'tubes' which slid one into the other. With a little effort he was able to slide them apart so that the frame increased in size until it fell apart. In fact these frames were adjustable, to fit a range of picture sizes.

Ingenious.

But it dawned on him that there could be a great deal more to his discovery than that. At long last he thought that he knew what Lina's picture scam was all about.

Collis had shown him Lina's most recent purchases only after they had been removed from their frames.

On his mobile he spoke to the police van and was lucky enough to find someone there. It was DC Potter.

'I'm at the studio – Collis's place, and I want you over here now.'

A fresh angle. And he told himself that it was one which should have occurred to him when the economics of the picture dealing were first questioned. Everybody knows about Amsterdam where banned drugs are available like sweets. They are not, of course, but that is the image. Now he had to decide what to do. There would have to be a forensic examination of the frames. Probably nothing would come of it but it had to be done. The Drugs Squad must be immediately involved. That sounded impressive, but the squad comprised only DS Boyd and three DSs. Of course they worked closely, and sometimes amicably, with Customs and Excise.

He recalled the starred entries which Iris Thorne had found in

Francine's diaries. He had been satisfied that they concerned Lina's picture transactions, but was it also possible that Francine had some notion of what she was really up to?

Potter arrived and was briefed. The fifteen-stone Potter in place of a police seal. 'Nobody to be admitted except on my say-so. I'll see that you're relieved as soon as possible.'

Wycliffe had reassembled the sections of the frame and he took it with him as he walked down the slope to Archer's office.

He needed to be careful. It was still possible – just – that the frames were no more than what they seemed to be, an ingenious device for accommodating pictures of different sizes.

The office was empty but it was not long before Archer arrived in answer to the bell. The Eric Gill image had faded and now the man looked almost frail, at least weighed down. He stood behind his desk, waiting for Wycliffe to speak.

Wycliffe laid the assembled frame on the desk top. Archer merely glanced at it, and all he said was, 'So you've got there.' He sounded relieved.

'You knew?'

Archer nodded. 'I've known since Tuesday afternoon. Three days. And it feels like for ever.'

Wycliffe said, 'We must be quite clear about this, Mr Archer. Are you saying that since Tuesday afternoon you have known that your wife was regularly importing illegal drugs concealed in the special frames of the pictures she bought in Amsterdam?'

'Yes, that is what I am saying.'

'How did you find out?'

Archer clasped his hands on the desk top. 'She told me.' The words were informed with an intense bitterness and he repeated them. 'She told me.'

Outside there was the mist and in the little office the light was dim. Wycliffe experienced a sense of unreality, of detachment, as though he was a spectator rather than a participant in the drama.

Archer went on, 'I think you must have realised, Mr Wycliffe, that Lina and I were not compatible. We had different views on almost everything and, in particular, on how the Guild should be run . . . The long and short of it is, of course, that I should never have married an Arian.'

A lengthy pause, then, 'It was early in April that I began to be really worried; worried about the way things seemed to be going. I was concerned about Collis in particular. Emile was becoming increasingly disturbed and his mysterious absences were more frequent.'

Archer shifted vigorously in his chair. 'For some time I had been aware that there was some sort of special relationship between him and Lina which I could not understand. Collis and Lander were known to be involved in a homosexual affair and for that reason, if for no other, it seemed unlikely that Lina . . . '

Wycliffe said nothing and eventually Archer resumed. 'In the end I tackled Emile and although he told me nothing, it was obvious that he was frightened of Lina, that she had some sort of hold over him. Of course, this only increased my worries and it became clear that my wife and Collis, and possibly Lander, were involved in some activity of which I knew nothing.'

Archer sat back in his chair looking directly at Wycliffe. 'To test the ground I suggested that we should get rid of Lander. After all, he was not even a member of the Guild, and she had often spoken of him with a certain contempt.

'But Lina would not hear of it, and when I pressed her she became angry.'

Archer removed his spectacles and began to polish them with a large handkerchief. 'On Tuesday afternoon we had, for the first time in our lives together, a real row. In the course of it she told me, quite deliberately, and in detail, what was going on. She seemed to take pleasure in shocking me. And in the end she said, "Now you can do what you like about it." '

There was another lengthy silence before he added, as though to himself, 'Of course, she knew me well enough to know that I would do nothing.'

'But you must have known that this put a quite different complexion on the murder of Francine Lemarque.'

Archer played nervously with his spectacles before putting them

147

back on, then he said, 'Lina was my wife. Everything depended . . . Everything! But you must understand that I did not believe for one moment, and I cannot believe now, that Lina was in any way responsible for the girl's death.'

Wycliffe said, 'When, on Wednesday morning, you reported that your wife was missing, you made no mention of the row on Tuesday afternoon. You spoke of an evening meal together and of separating to go to your rooms to work at around half-past eight as though your relationship was quite normal.'

Archer looked down at his hands. 'What I described to you was the usual pattern of our days. On Tuesday there was no evening meal. I have to admit that after the row I did not see Lina alive again.'

'Was Evadne Penrose aware of the quarrel?'

'No. It happened that she had some medical appointment and she left after lunch. In fact that was why I decided to bring things to a head just then.'

Wycliffe changed the subject. 'Do you know the nature of the drugs that were smuggled in the frames?'

'Oh yes. Lina made a point of keeping nothing back. It was heroin.'

Archer looked up, his manner resigned and bleak. 'What will happen to me now? I suppose that I am guilty of concealing a crime.'

Wycliffe had no wish to pursue that line. He had already decided that the interview had gone far enough; that further questioning would have to be formal, and a matter of record.

He said, 'You will be taken to Penzance Police Station where you will be interviewed formally and given an opportunity to make a statement which will be recorded.'

'Shall I be under arrest?'

'No. And you are, of course, free to seek legal advice and to be represented if you think that is necessary.'

Then, to make sure that the perspective was right, he added, 'You must understand that my main concern is still with the murders of Francine Lemarque and your wife.'

*

Back in the van, where he was alone, he telephoned Kersey and brought him up to date, then he called DS Boyd at headquarters.

'I want you down here, Tim . . . Say, with one of your team to start with. You might update your briefing on the present scene in the Plymouth, Exeter and Torbay areas beforehand . . . It's heroin, as I understand it. At the moment I've no information about quantity or quality but it comes from Amsterdam in hollow picture frames carried as air freight . . . Yes, this seems to have been going on for at least a couple of years . . . Once you've got the picture we must have early liaison with Customs. We've got a double murder inquiry on our hands and I can't afford to have our chaps swanning off to Amsterdam . . . I may not be around tomorrow until later in the day but Mr Kersey and Lucy Lane will be fully briefed.'

With Boyd in the picture Wycliffe tried to sort out his own ideas and get some kind of perspective. He recalled Iris Thorne's work on the starred entries in Francine's diaries and turned up the file in search of her report. Somebody, probably Lucy, had transformed the heap of papers which had littered the table into a file, and in it he found the report.

The first of Francine's stars in each case corresponded with Lina's return from Amsterdam. The second referred to the arrival of the pictures she had bought at auction. The significance of the third star against each first Friday following a delivery of the pictures had remained in question.

Could it be that the drugs, having been removed from the picture frames, were dispatched on these days?

It was an attractive idea and it occurred to him to wonder if these Fridays corresponded with Lander's alleged visits to his parents. Was Lander, with his motorbike, the courier?

He reminded himself that the transfer of payments up the line in these transactions was often a complicated and hazardous business: another problem for Boyd.

Lucy Lane arrived in time to play her usual role – to listen, then to put his thoughts into her own words with any comments she deemed appropriate.

She listened and then said her piece: 'So it's heroin rather than pictures. That makes sense. Tell me if I've got this straight. In Amsterdam Lina had her pictures reframed in hollow plastic, stuffed with packaged heroin. Presumably this would be the pure drug. At this end it would have to be removed from the frames, mixed with a high proportion of adulterants, and repackaged for the market. At the moment you are inclined to think that Collis was responsible for all this and that Lander was the errand boy who had the necessary contacts among the distributors.'

Lucy broke off. 'Is that how you see it?'

Wycliffe grinned. 'I do now.' A brief pause, then, 'If Collis really was responsible for unpacking the frames and adding the adulterants, presumably he did the work in his studio. Which means that there must be another forensic examination of his frame workshop possibly in conjunction with Customs, but that will be up to Boyd.'

Wycliffe tried to get comfortable on his bench and decided that it was not possible. He said to Lucy, 'So far you haven't mentioned the two murders.'

'No, I haven't. Well, on the face of it Collis seems to be our number-one suspect. Francine let him see that she knew too much and she was dealt with, presumably by him; then Lina put him under such pressure that he cracked. It doesn't take much imagination to reconstruct the probable sequence of events during the studio encounter on Tuesday night.'

Wycliffe said nothing and Lucy asked, 'You go along with that?'

'I can't see much in the way of an alternative. But I don't like it.'

A moment or two later he said, 'Did you get any lunch?'

'No.'

'Neither did I. Shall we see what Phyllis can do for us? The interview with Archer is at four and I want you to be there.'

'You won't be?'

'No, and I'm leaving Mr Kersey and you to deal with Boyd. I want to get home this evening. And look in at the office in the morning for a word with Mr Scales. Things are getting a bit hectic back there.'

Detective Chief Inspector John Scales was a long-term friend and colleague. A wizard at administration, it was he who made it possible for Wycliffe to spend so much time away from the office.

Lucy said, 'You know that tomorrow is Saturday?'

'That's the point; it will be quiet. As things stand, apart from those involved in the drug business, I'm inclined to call a halt for the weekend. It will give as many of the team as possible a break and, incidentally, help to rescue our budget. What's left of it. I'll have a word with Mr Kersey.'

But Man only proposes.

Four o'clock in an interview room at the police station: the tiny window of parboiled glass let in a minimum of light from the misty gloom outside. This competed with rather than supplemented the yellow glow from a low-wattage bulb.

'Present: Mr Francis Bacon Archer, Detective Chief Inspector Kersey and Detective Sergeant Lane. This interview is timed at sixteen-hundred hours and it is being recorded.' Lucy recited the obligatory preface.

Archer had groomed himself for the occasion: his beard had been trimmed, his long, greying hair was set in its silky waves. In appearance at least something of the Eric Gill image was restored. To sustain it he wore a black jerkin and dark grey trousers.

Kersey, as usual, looked the epitome of a traditional hard-faced cop, and Archer was clearly uneasy. The genus was probably unfamiliar.

Kersey pushed away the papers in front of him. 'I gather that you were concerned about Collis before Francine Lemarque was murdered.'

'Yes, I was puzzled by his manner – he was so edgy and tense and he seemed to get worse as time went on.'

'Did you connect this is any way with the girl?'

Archer stroked his beard. 'To some extent. I knew that Francine was stirring up a certain amount of resentment by her questions. As I saw it, she was no more than a source of mild irritation and I had no idea why what she was doing should upset Collis or anybody else at all seriously.'

'And then Francine was murdered.'

Archer raised his large pale hands. 'That was terrible! And totally inexplicable. I mean, I couldn't imagine what she could possibly have found out that threatened anyone; let alone something that could drive them to murder.'

Kersey leaned forward in his chair, arms on the table, his face close to Archer's. Off-putting, but Archer held his ground. Kersey said, 'That was on Sunday. And on Tuesday afternoon you quarrelled with your wife and in the course of that quarrel she told you exactly what was going on. Did that change your mind?'

Archer took his time, then in a low voice he said, 'I couldn't help seeing that there must be some connection.'

'Did she directly implicate Collis?'

'Yes, of course she did. She— '

'And Lander?'

Archer hesitated and Kersey gave him time. 'It was because of my tentative suggestion that we should get rid of Lander that we quarrelled. Lina didn't say how he was involved but it was obvious that he was.' Archer broke off. 'And he's gone, hasn't he? Just as Collis has gone.'

Archer, plaintive, added, 'I told all this to Mr Wycliffe.'

'And now you're telling it to the tape. Anyway, you said nothing and did nothing about what you had learned from your wife.'

There were little beads of perspiration on Archer's nose. 'What could I do or say – just like that? . . . At least I needed time to think and a chance to talk calmly with my wife. I decided to wait until the morning when Lina also would have had a chance to think more calmly.'

'But it turned out to be too late to talk to her.'

'Yes.'

'And Collis had gone.'

'Yes.'

'Do you have any idea where Collis might have gone? Where he spent the time he was away from the Guild site?'

'*No* idea at all. I wish to God I had.'

Kersey sat back in his chair. 'For the record, I want you to give an account in as much detail as you can remember of what exactly you did, saw and heard from the time at which you and your wife separated after the quarrel until you reported her missing the following morning.' Kersey broke off. 'Are you willing to do that?'

'I'll do my best.'

'Good! DS Lane will look after you.' Kersey turned to Lucy Lane. 'I'll send a PC to stand in.'

Kersey had had enough.

At just after five o'clock Wycliffe set out for home. He left the mist behind at Hayle and arrived at the Watch House in early evening sunshine. The estuary at full flood looked sleek and shining and smug. Helen was in the garden, dead-heading azaleas.

They got through those few moments of unease which are inevitable when two people who are close come together again after a spell of separation.

'I wasn't expecting you.'

'I know.'

'There's nothing in the house.'

'A crust of bread and thou . . . '

Helen giggled; an unusual phenomenon. 'You are a fool, Charlie Wycliffe! But I quite like you in small doses.'

Chapter Eleven

Saturday

At shortly before nine Wycliffe drove into the city, to police headquarters. There, the weekend had taken over. The desk officer was reading the sports pages of his *Mirror*, the lifts were being serviced, and the cleaners were loose on the stairs. (In sub-stations it would have been very different, with officers preparing for the weekend's wild men.)

But Wycliffe joined John Scales in the latter's office, and for the next two hours they discussed cases on hand, CID politics and their probable future under the new management.

Back in his own office he found Diane.

'Can't keep away?'

Diane had been with him long enough to graduate from eye-catching youth into a distinguished early middle-age. Never a man in sight.

She said, 'I thought you might turn up but there's plenty for me to do here. Anyway, mother's got her friends in and it will be one of those mornings. I'm better out of it.' She went on, 'As you're here, I'd like you to go through the assessments file with me. The chief will be asking for it when she gets settled in.'

'Have you seen much of her?'

'Very little. I'll get the file.'

They worked through the rest of the morning and had a canteen lunch, rather pleased with themselves.

It was half-past two when Wycliffe crossed the bridge once more into Cornwall and proceeded comfortably down the A30 to pick up the mist again at Hayle. Either it had been there since he left or this was a return visit. If anything it was denser than before.

He drove directly and with his usual caution to the Guild site and found Lucy Lane in the van drinking plastic-cup coffee while filing the latest house-to-house reports.

It occurred to him that his relationships with Diane and with Lucy had much in common. And perhaps Helen should be included. Three women who contrived to manage him without appearing to? He didn't care for the sound of that. So perhaps it was as well not to look at such matters too closely.

'Well?'

Lucy pushed her papers away. 'Tim Boyd is in the studio with his DC and a chap from Customs who specialises in narcotics. I put Tim in the picture and left them to it. Otherwise, nothing to report.'

Wycliffe helped himself to coffee from the machine, while outside the mist still blotted out that other world.

'I'll go and have a word.'

He was greeted by DS Boyd, lean, bony and dark. A man whose every movement had a quick, bird-like precision. Boyd was a phenomenon. His work in the Drugs Squad had developed into a campaign pursued with almost religious fervour. Boyd's eighteen-year-old daughter had died as a result of a single experiment with Ecstasy and following the tragedy Wycliffe had wondered whether he should continue in the job. But his intense hatred of importers, dealers and pushers had not so far affected his judgement, nor his responsibilities under the law.

Boyd was working with Doris Smale, one of his three DCs, and a grey-headed professorial-looking man from Customs whom Wycliffe did not know.

Boyd introduced him. 'David Blackwell – Detective Superintendent Wycliffe. David specialises in this field.'

A grave acknowledgement and David returned to an investigation of one of the cupboards, using a minute vacuum cleaner.

Boyd went on, 'No positive evidence yet, but it will come. It must be here and David will find it. No matter how thoroughly

Collis cleaned up he will have left traces of the adulterants if not of the actual drug.'

Boyd paused. 'Anyway, I can give you some idea of the quantities involved and they are significant.'

He picked up one of the adjustable plastic frames. 'I've looked at the last consignment of pictures and their average perimeter measurements work out at something over seventy inches. The hollow section of these frames has an area of almost exactly three-quarters of a square inch, so that the average picture offers a storage space of a little more than fifty cubic inches, say three hundred cubic centimetres if we go metric.'

Wycliffe could do without the arithmetic. 'What does that mean in terms of weight of heroin?'

Boyd frowned. 'Say a possible twenty-five ounces, or the best part of seven hundred grammes. In fact, I doubt if they would put in anything like that amount. It would probably be packed in polythene tubes to reduce the risk of possible leakage and betrayal, and not all the frames would be loaded. Even so it would not be difficult to make a good payload.'

'We are talking about pure heroin?'

'Oh yes. It wouldn't make much sense otherwise.'

'And you think the adulteration would have been carried out here. Knowing the current market, have you any idea of the probable extent of the adulteration?'

Boyd shrugged. 'Twenty times would be a minimum. There's very little smack on the market above the five per cent level . . . And it can easily go anywhere down to one per cent or even lower. The stuff we're finding at the moment in our area is in the three to four per cent range.'

'And the common adulterants?'

'Still the same. Almost anything goes. "Bulking out" as they call it is sometimes done with sugar or baking powder – even brick dust isn't unknown.'

'I'll leave you to it.'

Wycliffe had had his lesson which was in the nature of a revision course.

He walked back through the mist to the van, where Lucy had news for him.

'Mr Kersey's been on the line from the Incident Room. He's been approached by one of the local uniformed men who came off leave on the afternoon shift. A PC Laity. Laity saw the listing of Collis's car and though it's been recovered he had the sense to report that he might have come across it earlier. He has a friend who farms out in the sticks near Bodrifty, and he's pretty sure that he's seen Collis's car at intervals, over several months, parked outside a cottage not far away.

'At any rate he's sure it's a K-reg blue Peugeot 205 and he thinks that the index letters might include an A and a B.'

Wycliffe said, 'Worth taking a look at the place.' He called Kersey. 'Can you fix it for PC Laity to meet us at New Mill? . . . Say, in twenty minutes.'

'No problem. I'll have a word with his sergeant.'

Wycliffe turned to Lucy Lane. 'We'd better get moving.' He added, 'You can finish your coffee first.'

She gave him a look more eloquent than words and took her time. Looks are excluded from the disciplinary code.

Lucy drove with the screen-wipers working overtime. At New Mill, PC Laity materialised out of the fog.

'I got one of the patrol cars to drop me off, sir.'

Laity was fiftyish and grey, a shrewd man of a reflective turn of mind who thought before he spoke. Which was why his career would probably end more or less as it began.

In the car he pointed out the location on a map.

'Fine, but you'd better drive.'

Laity took over from Lucy Lane. 'We turn off within a few yards up into the moor.'

Lucy said, 'It was just beyond here that Collis's car was found abandoned.'

Laity said, 'Yes.'

Lucy tried again. 'So you know this part of the moor pretty well?'

'I'm learning. Billy Ward, who has a smallholding up there, is a

157

friend of mine and he's interested in the archaeology of the area. So we get around a bit. Bodrifty is on his doorstep.'

'Isn't that the Iron Age site where they found all that pottery?' Lucy, keeping her end up.

'They call it Iron Age and the excavated huts belong to that period but the pottery points to the site having been in continuous occupation at least from the Late Bronze, and probably up to the first century A D.'

There seemed to be no response to that so Lucy held her peace.

At a little distance beyond New Mill they turned off into the moor. A twisting uphill course through the mist, with no visible landmarks; then, abruptly, the mist would thin, with glimpses of the colours and contours of the moor, only to close in again almost at once.

Laity said, 'We are on the western slopes of Mulfra Hill. If you look at the map you'll see that we are surrounded by standing stones, Bronze Age field patterns, so-called "tumuli" and "settlements", and Mulfra Quoit is just up there on the hill.'

A moment or two later he added, almost apologetically, 'If you spend much time here it all comes alive.'

An odd policeman, and Wycliffe, who had said little, warmed towards him. Suddenly their preoccupation with the murder of two women had found its place in a pattern of four thousand years of human striving and endurance.

'There's Billy's place.'

A bleak little house of stone and slate with a few outbuildings backed on to a pattern of tiny Bronze Age fields. Only a pre-war tractor in an open shed even hinted at the present day.

Lucy Lane (BA: Eng. Lit.) said, 'Stella Gibbons must have been here.'

Wycliffe asked, 'Does your Billy make a living?'

Laity's answer to such a question marked the true Cornishman – a snub? 'He's still there.'

Then, remembering his manners and his company, 'Well, sir, that's where I've seen the blue Peugeot 205.'

Laity pointed to another house, built after the same fashion as

Billy's, but somewhat larger, with three windows upstairs instead of two and probably with more headroom inside. It was a hundred yards or so away, up a narrow stony track which ran between drystone walls.

They left the car at the bottom of the track and got out. Laity said, 'I'll fetch Billy if that's all right, sir.'

Billy was fiftyish, short, thick-set and dark, a possible and worthy successor to those Iron Age people who built and lived in the huts next door. He was attended by a suspicious black and white Collie.

Introductions over and the situation explained, Billy said, 'We never did more than pass the time of day and that not very often. He just came and went at all sorts of times and I can't say I took a lot of notice. I heard his name through the agent. He's called Collins, but that's about all I know.'

'Can you tell us anything about him? . . . Age? Looks?'

Billy frowned, 'Fortyish, slim, dark . . . A bit foreign-looking I thought.'

'Sounds like our man.'

Wycliffe led the way up to the other house. The place looked cared for. Even the cobbled path had been weeded. The front door and the window frames were painted blue and there were patterned curtains drawn over the single window on the ground floor.

Lucy put her hand on the door and it opened a little. She knocked but there was no response.

Wycliffe, recalling his childhood, said, 'Perhaps they don't lock up round here.'

Whenever his job took him into the private world of a stranger Wycliffe knew that same sense of anticipation and mild excitement which he experienced when opening the pages of a biography or journal for the first time. He was about to discover how somebody else had coped, or failed to cope, with this odd business of being alive.

They entered a room that ran the length of the cottage but it was a moment or two before their eyes accommodated to the dim light. The floor was made of slate slabs, worn and polished by generations of feet. There were rugs. The ceiling beams had been stained, and an oil lamp on an adjustable chain hung from one of them. The walls were colour-washed in sunshine yellow.

Apart from a couple of bookcases, a desk and a wall cupboard, the furniture consisted of a sturdy round table, kitchen chairs and a couple of comfortable-looking armchairs set by the open fireplace. The fireplace held a mass of burned paper which had spilled over into the fender and there was a slight but pervasive smell of decay. But in all other respects the room was a model of order and cleanliness.

To Wycliffe it spoke of a reclusive, fastidious man who had created for himself a refuge. And it fitted his image of Collis like a glove. If this was his hideaway, it came as no surprise.

But the walls were bare; not a picture in sight. And, oddly, that seemed to fit too.

Wycliffe often wondered how he would cope if he were ever left totally alone. Sometimes he imagined himself descending passively into squalor; at others he could see himself in a place of refuge like this, polished and sterile.

Behind the living room there was a lean-to kitchen, primitive but clean. No sink, no tap, no water laid on, but there was a bucket and dipper on the floor. Any cooking must have been done on an antique oil stove with a fretted top, or on the open fire in the living room.

'Look here!' Lucy sounded urgent. Wycliffe came out of the kitchen and joined her at the bottom of the stairs which were screened off from the room by a door which Lucy had opened. The smell of decay was now overpowering.

A man's body hung in the stairwell, suspended on a cord secured to a roof beam.

It was Collis. The slender build of the man, the dark hair in tight curls – even in the poor light there was no room for doubt. But the clothes were unfamiliar: a gaily patterned shirt, and tightly fitting plum-coloured trousers with matching socks. The body gyrated slowly in the gentle air currents, with the feet well clear of the middle stair. Wycliffe climbed the stairs, easing past the legs. 'He's been here quite a while . . . Nothing we can do . . . Poor devil!'

Never at ease with death in any circumstances, Wycliffe forced himself to look at the face he had last seen in life. Pale then, now it was livid; the eyes were open and they bulged slightly; the lips were parted, showing the teeth. A noose of nylon cord encircled the neck just below the chin but above the larynx. The cord was secured to a cross-beam in the unceiled roof.

This inanimate thing, dangling at the end of a rope, had, not very long since, been a man.

Poor Collis.

As the body rotated gently he saw that the hair at the base of the skull was bloodstained. A blow? Then he realised that if Collis had launched himself from the top step into the stairwell, the knot in the noose could have been wrenched up against the base of the skull in precisely that position.

He called down to Lucy, 'I'm going to take a look around upstairs.'

He glanced at his watch: it was half-past seven.

Upstairs there was not much to see: three rooms, one little more than a cupboard with a window. Only one of the rooms was furnished: a double bed, a marble-topped wash-stand with ewer and basin, and a wardrobe. The bed was made up and covered by a white counterpane, in keeping with the rest.

Over the bed, the only picture he had so far seen in the house, was a framed drawing, a superb pencil sketch of Francine, head and shoulders, in profile; and it was initialled EC.

Wycliffe joined Lucy downstairs. On his mobile he spoke to Kersey. 'We need the full crew, Doug. Looks like suicide but we need to be certain. You get hold of the police surgeon. I'll tackle Franks.'

To Lucy he said, 'Collis went off during Tuesday night, and it's now Saturday evening. Almost four days. We need to know how long he's been dead. Let's hope that Franks will be gracious enough to tell us.'

Wycliffe used his mobile again to speak to Franks. The pathologist was in a mood. 'Where is this place? It sounds like the back of bloody beyond.'

'It is. So if you can't read a map then drive to the Guild site and I'll arrange for somebody to pilot you the rest of the way.'

Outside, they joined PC Laity who was chatting with Billy Ward.

Wycliffe said, 'I'm afraid we have bad news for you, Mr Ward. Your neighbour has been dead for a matter of days.'

Billy looked shocked. 'I had no idea he was still there.'

'Did you see or hear anyone there on Tuesday night?'

'Tuesday night . . . ' Furrowed brow. 'Yes, it was Tuesday night. He woke me up in the small hours. I remember flashing my torch at the clock and it was just turned half-past one. He was driving off and I wondered where anybody could be going at that time of night.'

'You are sure that he was leaving, not arriving?'

'Of course I'm sure. I listened to the sound dying away in the distance.'

'You've no idea when he arrived at the cottage?'

'No. Except that he was there when I went to bed. I don't take much notice of comings and goings unless they happen to disturb me.'

Wycliffe said, 'I'm sorry to be persistent but this could be important. Do you feel reasonably sure that the car you heard leaving was the one belonging to your neighbour?'

'Unless it was one like it. Those little diesels make a row like a small truck.'

'Thank you, Mr Ward. You've been very helpful. Do you live here alone?'

'Ever since mother died.'

The troops were gathering. Posts and tapes were set up to create an exclusion zone. Wycliffe asked himself for whom? But it was routine. Fox, who always managed to appear rather than arrive, presented himself like a genie out of a bottle. His van and his assistant would be somewhere around.

'Any special instructions, sir?'

Forbes, the police surgeon, arrived and made his inspection. 'Obviously it's a job for Franks but to me it looks like a clear case of suicide. I'd guess that he's been there up to four days . . . Look, I'm supposed to be at the hospital. I shall get scalped. If you will apologise to Franks . . . '

Wycliffe talked to Fox: 'To start with we want the usual shots of the body with special attention to the noose and to the injury to the base of the skull. I leave the rest to you.'

Wycliffe felt unusually benevolent towards Fox. 'You thought it probable that Collis had a hideaway and here it is; so after the body has gone it's all yours. Obviously much that we might have wanted to see has been burned, but do what you can. See what you can make of it.'

Fox nodded wisely. 'I quite understand, sir.'

Forensic came next, in the person of 'Flo'. She came with her assistant and they were followed by the mortuary van. And finally, Franks, piloted by a PC, who looked pale, as well he might. Franks drove like Jehu of old, but Jehu had to make do with a chariot and a horse or two.

The area had probably not seen so many people gathered together in one place since the Bodrifty 'dig' and perhaps before that, when the 'old' people were still pasturing their sheep and their tiny oxen on the moor.

'Well, Charles? Let's get on with it!'

It was nine o'clock; the mist was clearing with the coming of dusk, and as it did so their little island expanded into the landscape of the moor. It was still chilly.

Franks climbed the stairs and spent some time examining the head and neck of the dead man while Wycliffe watched from below.

Franks said, 'You think he hanged himself?'

'That's how it looked to me.'

'How did he get the injury to the back of his neck?'

Wycliffe realised that he was being tempted on to thin ice and was cautious. 'I thought at first that it might have been the result of a blow but it occurred to me afterwards that if he had launched himself from the top of the stairs, the knot in the noose might have caused it.'

Franks muttered to himself, then, 'So he jumped – or *launched* himself, as you put it, from the top stair. Is that your version?'

'You tell me yours.' Wycliffe had had enough.

Franks came back down the stairs and into the living room. 'In the days when murderers were judicially hanged, how did they in fact die?'

'I'm listening.'

'Well, they weren't strangled by the noose: the sudden six-foot drop dislocated the cervical vertebrae and ruptured the spinal cord.'

Franks waited for the question which did not come, then went on, 'Your man was strangled by the noose. In my opinion there was no jump.'

'Are you saying— '

'I'm saying that he *could* have swung – not jumped – off the top of the stairs. In which case he *could* have been strangled *and* suffered injury to the base of his skull. I need to look into the nature and extent of that injury before I can give an opinion, and I can only do that when I've got him on the table.'

'You think the hanging could have been faked?' Wycliffe was shaken.

'I'll tell you what I think when I've established the facts.' Franks being Franksish.

'Anything to say about how long he's been dead?'

Franks pouted. 'It's a guess, but I'd say at least three days, probably longer.'

Half an hour later the body had been removed and was on its way to the mortuary. Franks had gone, but he would be unable to start on the autopsy until the body had been formally identified. In his present mood he might well delay a start until morning.

Wycliffe said, 'Now, Lucy. With no next-of-kin that we know of we shall have to find somebody from the Guild to do the ID. Archer is the obvious choice, but in all the circumstances he may not feel that he can do it. Anyway, there's nothing more for us here so let's leave it to the experts.'

It was agreed that Fox would attend to the recording of any evidence that might suffer from further delay, then pack it in until morning.

Wycliffe and Lucy Lane were driven back to the Guild site by Laity and, as they were about to get out of the car, Wycliffe turned to Laity. 'Are you willing to act as coroner's officer *pro tem?*'

Somebody had to shepherd and console the bereaved relatives or their stand-ins, and brief the coroner.

'I've done it a couple of times before, sir.'

'Good! We can regularise it in the morning. Now you'd better come with us to break the news to Archer.'

It was dark; the stars were out in a clear sky and lights twinkled around the site. There was only one light in the Archer house and it came from a window on the first floor.

'That's his room. I hope he hasn't gone to bed.'

Lucy rang the door bell and, after a lapse of time, a light came on in the hall and the door was opened.

It was not Archer but Evadne Penrose, in her dressing-gown. Her manner was subdued, almost apologetic. 'He's up in his room but whether he's gone to bed or not, I don't know. He's in a state, and I thought somebody ought to be in the house with him at night, so I stayed.' She broke off. 'Do I have to get him down?'

'I'm afraid so.'

'In that case you'd better come in.'

They waited in the little hall and eventually Archer arrived, fully dressed. He stood looking at them, silent and apprehensive.

'Is there somewhere we can talk?'

Without a word Archer led the way, not into the drawing room, but into the office. There, he seated himself behind his desk and let them find chairs for themselves.

'I suppose you have news of Emile.' His eyes were red-rimmed with tiredness and his hair and beard were unkempt. Archer was near the end of his tether.

Wycliffe told him the news.

'So Emile is dead.' He spoke very slowly. 'I was afraid that was what you had come to tell me.' His large pale hands, resting on the desk top, seemed to grope for something which they failed to find. 'It was suicide, of course.'

Wycliffe said nothing and Archer went on, 'I find it impossible to think of Emile killing anybody . . . But he was a Piscean, you know, Mr Wycliffe. Highly strung, nervous – easily led to a certain point . . . He had ability as a draughtsman – many Pisceans have artistic skills – but little *stamina*.' Archer shook his head. 'When I look back I realise that he must have felt hopelessly trapped . . . '

Wycliffe said, 'We do not know that he killed anyone. The autopsy will tell us exactly how he himself died, and our investigation will carry on from there. But before any of that can happen we have to have a formal identification of the body. And in the absence of relatives it needs to be done by someone who knew him well.'

Archer looked up. 'Are you suggesting that I might do it?'

'I shall fully understand if you decide that you cannot.'

Archer shook his head. 'On the contrary, whatever has happened, I feel that I must help you in your investigation in any way that I can.'

Wycliffe thanked him. 'In that case Constable Laity will acquaint you with the procedure and take you to the mortuary.'

On their way back to the hotel Lucy put the question of the moment: 'Well, what do we make of it? Collis was a fugitive, a murderer twice over. Frustrated in his efforts to get away, he decided to put an end to it. Is that our line?'

Wycliffe took his time. 'We can't have a line until Franks makes up his mind about the neck injury, and gives us his opinion as to whether or not Collis took his own life. All we've got to go on so far is the fact that Collis is dead, and Archer's revised version of what happened on Tuesday afternoon – and afterwards.

'According to him, he and his wife had a showdown on Tuesday afternoon and that was the last time he saw her alive. They did not have their usual evening meal together and they do not in any case share a bedroom. It was only when he had not seen her by ten o'clock on Wednesday morning, and her bed had not been slept in, that he went to consult Collis and found the studio locked and apparently deserted.

'At that point he came to us. And it was later that day when Collis's car was found abandoned on the Penzance side of New Mill.'

Wycliffe paused and took a deep breath. 'Along with all this we have Billy Ward's account of the little Peugeot leaving in the small hours. He doesn't know when Collis or anybody else arrived at the cottage. And there we have it.'

Wycliffe sighed. 'I suppose all this can be fitted together, but not by me – not tonight, anyway.'

They arrived back at the hotel.

Too late to ring Helen.

The night staff gave them sandwiches and, of all things, cocoa. 'It will help you sleep. No caffeine.'

But the recipe did not work for Wycliffe. And the Woolf Diary 1931–35 failed him too. At one o'clock he was still wrestling with permutations of the facts of the case as he could recall them. And always at the back of his mind was the memory of that pathetic body swaying gently in the air currents of the stairwell at the end of a nylon cord.

Collis and Lander both left the Guild site at some time on Tuesday night.

Together?

A good question.

And Lina Archer's body was found on the floor of Collis's studio next morning.

Billy Ward had his sleep interrupted by a car leaving in the small hours of Wednesday morning, and later Collis's abandoned car, out of fuel, was found at New Mill, at a point a little beyond the turning which led to his cottage.

Was Collis alone?

If it turned out that he had been murdered then obviously there must have been someone with him in the cottage. Had the car been abandoned by his killer?

And what about Lander in all this? Lander and his motorcycle were missing. Billy Ward had not mentioned a motorcycle. Had Lander been a regular visitor at the cottage?

It seemed more than likely. But, more to the point, was he there on Tuesday night? It was possible that Fox and Forensic might have something to say about that.

Wycliffe's thoughts processed in circles.

From time to time he had browsed in popular works on quantum theory and he could get himself into a similar sleep-destroying mode over the ambivalent life/death of Schrödinger's cat.

Chapter Twelve

Sunday

But sleep came at last, and the very next thing he knew was that the sun was shining into his room, and somewhere a church bell tolled. He didn't need the church bell to tell him that it was Sunday. Wycliffe was convinced that if he awoke after being unconscious for a week he would know if it was Sunday. There was something in the air, something in the rhythm of life – something, anyway. But Helen maintained that it was nonsense.

He looked at his bedside clock. Three minutes to seven.

On Sunday morning a week ago, admittedly a good deal later than this, he had been sitting in his garden at the Watch House, concentrating hard on thinking about nothing. Now that was seven days, and three deaths by violence, away.

The eight o'clock news carried a report of the finding of Collis's body: 'Following the two recent murders at the craft colony, known as the Guild of Nine, at St Ives in Cornwall, the police, last night, acting on information received, visited a remote cottage on the moor and discovered the body of Emile Collis, the Guild's painter. An investigation is under way to establish the circumstances in which Mr Collis met his death.

'A police spokesman refused to comment when asked if this discovery was likely to bring closer a solution to the mystery surrounding these crimes.'

Wycliffe had been successful so far in holding back news of the drug trafficking, for fear of putting suspects on their guard and driving them underground.

Downstairs the 'Sundays' were displayed in the hotel vestibule and 'The Guild Murders' had made the front page of one of the tabloids with a photograph in full colour of the interior of Archer's nonogon under a caption 'Boardroom for Death?' Somebody must have turned a blind eye.

Wycliffe had breakfast with Kersey and Lucy Lane. In view of the latest development Kersey had cancelled his day at home with the family. He would remain in charge of the Incident Room while Wycliffe and Lucy Lane worked from the van on the site. Scene of Crime would resume at Collis's cottage but routine inquiries had been suspended to save money on overtime.

At shortly before nine, in the Incident Room, Wycliffe had a call from Franks. The pathologist was in ebullient mood. 'I was right, Charles!'

Wycliffe refrained from pointing out that as he hadn't given an opinion one way or the other he could hardly be wrong.

'So?'

'The injury to the base of the skull was certainly aggravated by the knot in the noose. Whether the knot *caused* the injury is another matter. There *could* have been a blow to that area but it's now impossible to say that there was. In my opinion *if* there was such a blow it did not break the skin but it could have been sufficient to cause insensibility.'

'In fact, you don't know whether Collis hung himself or was hanged.'

'I'm afraid that is so. If I'd been called in even twenty-four hours earlier I could have been more definite.'

Wycliffe dispensed sympathy. 'We must try to give you better notice in future. Unfortunately we don't know that we've got a corpse until we find it.

'Anyway, in your view, we could be dealing with suicide or murder.'

'Yes. Collis could have put the cord around his own neck and swung out over the stairs. As I said before, there could be no question of a jump. That would have resulted in dislocation of the cervical vertebrae of which there is no trace.'

Franks had not finished. '*If* it was murder, it could have been a repeat of what happened to the woman. She was bludgeoned, then strangled, but in her case there was no attempt to make it look like a suicide.'

'Anything else?'

'Since you ask me – yes. Our man could have been involved in a bit of a struggle. There was a certain amount of light scratching to the face. It is conceivable that an attacker tried to stop him crying out, but it could have been nothing of the sort. It might have happened earlier – when and if he killed the woman.'

'Is that it?'

'No, there is something else that may be worth mentioning. There were a few spots of blood on the front of Collis's shirt. It is unlikely but I suppose they could have come from the wound at the base of his skull, or even from the scratches to his face. On the other hand, it's just possible they belonged to somebody else. Anyway, Forensic have his clothing and I've asked them to take a look, so I expect you will be hearing from them.

'That is it, unless you want to know that he has all his teeth with only two fillings, that he had a slightly enlarged spleen— '

'I can do without that.'

'Good! I'll let you have my report. But, Charles, do try not to be so bloody awkward. Life is too short.'

Wycliffe replaced the telephone with commendable restraint and spoke mildly. 'Franks can be extremely irritating without even trying.'

He passed on the news to Lucy. 'We seem to get in deeper and deeper . . . We must bring in Lander.'

'You think— '

'I've given up thinking.'

It was an odd feature of this case that at each stage he had found some reason (or excuse) to talk to Marsden. It was not that he had any suspicion of the man and he was certainly not, or so he told himself, seeking advice, but half an hour spent in the old reprobate's company seemed to broaden his perspective.

He said to Lucy, 'Join me at the Guild site in an hour, and then we'll see what Fox is up to.'

Sunday morning. The road to Mulfra was almost deserted, the sun shone, the bell of Mulfra church tolled, and it was possible to believe in almost anything.

He turned down the lane past the Tributers' and parked near Marsden's cottage where the track was wide enough. Marsden's door was open and music blasted out across the valley. Classed as 'spiky music' in Wycliffe's technical vocabulary, it had long since been dismissed by him as 'modern stuff' by composers with unpronounceable Russian names.

He stepped over Percy, asleep in the sunshine, and went in.

'What do you want? I'm busy.' Marsden's voice came from the studio . . . 'Oh, it's you.'

Marsden was at work on a blocked-in painting of the cove, with Mynhager in the foreground.

'A commission. Woman who used to live round here wants a pretty picture to hang on her wall to remind her of times past. A photo would do her just as well but this will keep Percy in cat food for a bit.'

He suspended operations, attended to his brushes and palette, then joined Wycliffe in the living room. 'Have you found Collis?'

'You haven't listened to your radio. We found him last night.' Wycliffe described the circumstances and Marsden seemed genuinely distressed. 'Poor EC! I'm really sorry. We had a couple of good years together and what makes it worse is that it was I who got him mixed up with Lina.' He broke off. 'I suppose he put an end to it himself?'

'We don't know. Franks says it's too long since death for him to give a firm opinion. It's possible that he was rendered insensible by a blow to the base of the skull and then strung up in a fake suicide, but Franks won't commit himself.'

Marsden was shocked. 'But what *is* this? You can't tell me that there've been three killings over some fiddle with a few bloody paintings that were hardly worth bringing in anyway. It doesn't make sense.'

'The pictures were a cover for drugs.'

Marsden looked blank. 'But how? I still don't see— '

'They arrived framed.'

'So?'

'The frames were hollow and it seems that they were stuffed with pure heroin.'

Marsden was incredulous. 'I can't believe . . . The clever bitch! . . . I knew that she was greedy with no holds barred: that's one reason why I kept clear of her bloody Guild. But this!'

And a moment later: 'So where did EC come in?'

'As far as we can tell, he dealt with the unpacking, bulking-up and repacking, plus the reframing of the pictures; all carried out in his studio, presumably by him, possibly with Lander's assistance.'

Wycliffe had never seen Marsden so agitated. 'Poor bugger! EC could never say "No" and stick to it. She could twist him round her little finger.'

He was silent for a while, then, 'But even so these killings don't fit . . . I mean, even if she's cut in on the big boys they wouldn't risk drawing attention to themselves with this kind of mayhem. It doesn't add up.'

Wycliffe had got what he wanted: his own ideas put into words by somebody who also knew something of life on the other side. He said, 'What I've told you is confidential for the moment.'

Marsden grinned. 'My lips are sealed.'

'They'd better be.'

He drove back to the Guild site and joined Lucy in the van. As usual Marsden had helped him to orientate his thinking and he needed to talk.

'We are dealing with three deaths by violence, Lucy: Francine, Lina and Collis; three murders, or two murders and a suicide, because it's still possible that Collis killed the other two and then took his own life.'

Lucy said, 'Forensic could help us there if they are able to identify the source of the bloodstains on Collis's shirt.'

'Yes. And all we can do about that is to keep our fingers crossed. But there's another point. It's not only a question of "who?" but also, of "why?" It seems to me that the motives behind the killings of Francine and Lina were almost certainly different. Presumably Lina died, at the hands of Collis or another, as a direct result of her involvement in the picture scam. But what about Francine? There is really nothing to suggest that she knew anything of significance about what was going on. She was inquisitive, but Francine was inquisitive about anything that might affect her involvement with the Guild.'

Lucy agreed. 'In any case, she would have been more likely to have involved herself than go for exposure.' Lucy had a less favourable view of Francine than Wycliffe. 'But are you saying that we may be dealing with two killers?'

Wycliffe hesitated, 'No, that would be incredible. Anyway, we shan't get any further by talking. Let's see what Fox is up to at the cottage.'

Lucy drove to New Mill then up on to the moor and through deserted lanes to Collis's refuge.

In sunshine the bleak little cottages looked out of place. Billy Ward was pegging out his washing and the Scene of Crime van was parked outside Collis's cottage.

Lucy said, 'All right if I have a word with Billy? I've a feeling that we might not have got all he has to tell us.'

'Good idea. See what you can do. And sound him out on motorbikes. I'll deal with Fox.'

Fox greeted him at the door.

The room looked just as Wycliffe had last seen it except that the grate had been cleared of burned paper and Fox's current assistant, a young DC, was seated at the table sorting through a heap of charred paper fragments with forceps and probe. Promising fragments were placed between sheets of polythene for later examination by a specialist.

Over the years Fox had had a succession of assistants, all out of the same mould: male, youngish, largely mute and incredibly long-suffering.

Wycliffe gave him the news from Franks and Fox received it without any great surprise. 'So he could have been murdered. I've a gut feeling that he didn't do all this himself with suicide in mind. I mean, why bother?

'Anyway, somebody burned all this and the bulk of it isn't going to tell us much. Hicks is sorting out the fragments, and so far they confirm what I said. Collis kept all his personal stuff here and not at his studio; not only documents, but letters, and the sort of things people keep in drawers which they never open. He seems to have kept a diary or journal at some time in a hard-covered exercise book, but it was ripped to pieces before being thrown on the fire with the rest.'

Wycliffe said, 'Anything you've got on his visitors here is going to be useful.'

Fox stroked his bony chin, his most conspicuous feature next to the length of his legs. 'He certainly had one regular visitor and that was Lander. Lander's prints are all over the place, just as they were in the studio flat.'

'Any recent?'

Fox hesitated. 'I gather from what you said that Collis probably died on Tuesday night. All I can say is that, from the prints I've found, it's *possible* that Lander was around as recently as that.'

'Other visitors?'

'There were others: two other males, unidentified so far. They were not frequent visitors and their prints are confined to this room.'

Fox summed up: 'I've no doubt at all that this is where the man really *lived*, but somebody has systematically set about destroying everything that might have told us anything about him and his background.'

'And he could have done that himself in preparation for clearing out but it is possible that he was murdered first.'

'As you say, sir.' Fox added, uncharacteristically, 'I feel sorry for the poor devil.'

Wycliffe said, 'Don't forget that he must have played a role in the drug racket.'

Fox made a dismissive gesture. 'Women! They can make a man do anything. I reckon the Bible story got it just about right but the fig leaves were too late and too few.'

Wycliffe said, 'But it's pretty obvious that Collis was gay.'

'In my opinion, as often as not, that can be an escape route. Anyway, sir, you want to know what I've found, and it amounts to very little so far. We may have something when Hicks has finished playing with his bits of burned paper but I doubt it.'

Wycliffe was intrigued by this unique insight into Foxian philosophy. The records showed that Fox was married but nobody seemed to know anything of his life away from the job.

'When do you expect to finish here?'

'I should be through by this evening.'

'Morning, miss. What can I do for you?' Billy picked up his empty clothes basket. 'Nice day for drying. You don't get too many o' them up here. That's why you find me washing on a Sunday.'

'I'm DS Lane.'

'I know you're police, I saw you here last night. Funny job for a woman I always think. But there; times change. You'd best come in.'

Billy led the way into his kitchen which was also his living room: stone floor, mats and, wonder of wonders, a Cornish cooking range. Must be one of the last in use, Lucy thought. Basic furniture plus well-filled bookshelves. On the mantelshelf above the range there was a row of pots, some of them with bits missing.

'They came from the dig. They let me keep 'em as souvenirs. And I've got quite a little collection of sherds and other oddments which I keep in drawers.'

Billy's collie came to inspect her, then settled on the mat in front of the range, forepaws thrust out, tail tucked away.

Lucy said, 'I suppose you get quite a few visitors through your interest in archaeology, and having Bodrifty on your doorstep.'

'Too many sometimes. Come July an' August they can be a nuisance.'

'Do you ever see anybody from the Guild?'

A smile. 'I thought we might be getting there, miss. I've had the potter up here a couple of times – Scawn, that's his name. Very knowledgeable chap. It does a man good to see him handle a pot.

He even smells it. You can see that he's back with whoever made it. In tune like.'

'Anyone else?'

'Archer himself came here once. Not about pots. He wanted to talk about the old people's interest in astrology.'

'And were they interested?'

'Perhaps, but in a more practical way than the stuff he believes in. His ideas came from out East much later; along with a lot of other funny notions.'

Lucy decided to get down to basics. 'It's possible that your neighbour didn't hang himself, Mr Ward. He could have been murdered.'

Billy was shocked. 'Oh dear! That is nasty! . . . Murdered . . . Poor man!'

The old wall clock with a yellowing face ticked away the better part of a minute before he went on, 'Now I see what you're after, but I'm afraid that what I can tell you won't get you far.'

'Did either of your visitors from the Guild show any interest in your neighbour?'

Billy pursed his lips. 'Not that I recall . . . If they did, I don't remember, but I wouldn't have thought much about it anyway.'

'Did your neighbour have a visitor who came on a motorbike?'

Billy nodded. 'Oh, he's a regular, and he's sometimes there overnight.'

'Can you say when you last saw him?'

A smile. 'I don't think I *saw* much of him at all, and when I did he had his helmet on, but I heard him all too often. That bike of his is enough to wake the dead. He hasn't been around for a few days.'

'Can you recall the last time you heard him?'

'I know it was evening . . . ' He considered. 'That's right. I was having a bit of a clean-up in the barn an' that's a Tuesday job. So it must've bin Tuesday. He didn't stay long that time. I remember I was still working in the barn when he left.'

Lucy prompted. 'You told us that it was Tuesday when you heard Collis's little Peugeot being driven off in the middle of the night.'

Billy looked concerned. 'So I did. But I never connected the two. You wouldn't, would you? You're asking me about things that didn't seem to matter at the time, and then you don't take much notice.'

Lucy was appreciative. 'I quite understand. You've been very helpful.'

She left to rejoin Wycliffe in Collis's cottage.

Wycliffe said, 'So Lander was here on Tuesday but, according to Billy, he didn't stay long. All the same, we need to find him.'

Back at the site there was a curious feeling of suspended animation. It was a Sunday, but they had been told that Sundays made little difference to the routine. If there still was a routine.

As they left the car and walked towards the police van they were joined by Archer, looking almost dishevelled. His hair was unbrushed and his beard untrimmed; his glasses had slipped, apparently unnoticed, halfway down his nose. 'You've had a report on Emile's death?'

Wycliffe said, 'It's inconclusive. The pathologist says that he can't decide whether or not Collis died by his own hand.'

They had stopped in a little group by the van. It seemed that Archer had more to say but had difficulty in finding the words. 'You've been to the cottage?'

'We've just come from there. Our people are still in possession.'

Archer shook his head. 'I didn't even know that he had a cottage.'

They had lunch at the Tributers' where Phyllis, with two assistants – girls from the village – still had her work cut out. A fine warm Sunday brought out the trippers. Wycliffe and Lucy turned down the roast chicken that was most in demand and went for a salad.

They were less than halfway through their meal when Wycliffe's bleeper bleeped and he went outside to take the call.

DC Potter, on duty at the Incident Room. 'Sorry to disturb you, sir, but I've just received a message from PC Foster at the Guild site. He says that a chap has turned up there, on a motorbike, claiming to be Robert Lander. He wants to talk to you and he won't talk to anyone else. Foster says there was something odd about the man and he even had doubts about his identity – thought he might be some nutter. But the potter, Scawn, happened to see him and he had no doubt, though he seemed anything but pleased to see him again.'

Wycliffe said, 'Make sure they hold on to him and tell them I'll be along.'

Back in the Tributers' he passed the news to Lucy. He was disturbed. 'We have the whole police force supposed to be looking out for this man and he turns up of his own accord, on our doorstep, on his bike. Is he trying to take the mickey or something? At any rate we'd better get over there.'

Lucy said, 'Aren't you going to finish your lunch?' And then, 'Remember Drake? . . . And Lander isn't exactly the Armada.'

Wycliffe grinned. 'One of these days, Lucy . . . ' But he went on with his meal.

They found Lander in the police caravan on the Guild site, drinking coffee, apparently self-possessed and relaxed. By contrast, his watchdog, PC Foster, seemed tense and had placed himself between Lander and the door.

'You have met us both before: Detective Superintendent Wycliffe and Detective Sergeant Lane.' Wycliffe was not quite sure of the line to take, so he opened with a question which would set the man talking. 'Why have you come back?'

Lander looked surprised. 'Because I heard this morning on the radio that Emile was dead.'

'And that meant something to you?'

'It meant a very great deal to me. Emile and I were very close friends . . . More than that.'

'Lovers?'

'Yes.'

Lander was as Wycliffe remembered him: the tall, muscular blond with the pudding-basin haircut.

'Where were you this morning?'

'In Torquay. I've been there since I left here, staying with a friend. How exactly did Emile die?'

'I'll answer your questions when you have answered some of mine. You knew that you were wanted for questioning in connection with these crimes?'

'No. I did not! I had no idea.'

'But you managed to get here without being picked up by our people.'

Lander patted his hair. 'Well, with this lot under a helmet I don't suppose there's much to see and my bike is much like other people's. Anyway, I wasn't picked up.'

Wycliffe looked at him steadily without speaking, then, 'Are you a congenital liar, Mr Lander?'

A faint smile. 'That's laying it on a bit. I make up stories.'

'About your relationship with Derek Scawn, about the parents you found it convenient to visit from time to time '

Lander looked positively sheepish. 'I've done that sort of thing since I was a child, Mr Wycliffe. When things were not as I would have liked them to be I've pretended that they were different. But as far as I know I've never harmed anyone in my life.'

'So how does it come about that you are now wanted for questioning in connection with possibly three murders, and offences under the Dangerous Drugs Acts?'

Lander was looking at Wycliffe with total incomprehension. 'But I – I don't understand. I've done nothing – nothing! Then after a brief pause, 'You said *three* murders . . . '

'It's possible that your friend Emile Collis was murdered.'

Lander looked stunned.

'When you heard that he was dead you thought that he must have taken his own life – is that it?'

'Of course!'

Wycliffe still could not make up his mind whether Lander's concern was genuine or all part of the act. '*If* what you now say is true I think the time has come for you, in your own interest, to be totally honest about what you know and the part you have had in what has happened.'

'I'll do my best.'

Lander, like Wycliffe and Lucy Lane opposite him, was wedged on a narrow seat by the fixed table, but he contrived somehow to strike an attitude, conveying total openness and transparency.

'You knew that, under cover of importing pictures, Lina was engaged in smuggling illegal drugs, and that Emile was involved?'

'Yes, I knew.'

'How did you find out?'

Lander ran long fingers through his blond hair. 'Pillow talk. Emile was becoming increasingly edgy and depressed, and in the end I got him to talk. He was the sort to find himself in a mess without realising how he'd got there, and he desperately wanted out. I suggested that we should go off together but he wouldn't hear of it. He had some crackpot idea of making Lina see the error of her ways . . . I'm afraid I lost patience.'

'In all this Collis referred to Lina as though she were still alive?'

'Of course.'

'Were you in any way involved with the drug trafficking?'

'No, I was not.'

'Are you saying that you did not act as Lina's courier, taking her drugs to market?'

For the first time Lander reacted with vigour. 'I most certainly am saying exactly that!'

'Did Emile discuss with you any of the details of Lina's dealings?'

'In so far as he knew them. He knew nothing of the monetary transactions, although he admitted that Lina paid him well.'

'If you didn't act as courier do you know how the drugs reached the distributors?'

Lander smiled. 'It was by courtesy of the Royal Mail. They were sent in smallish packages by book post.' He shook his head. 'Lina was a clever witch. She'll haunt whoever killed her, that's for sure.'

Wycliffe glanced at Lucy Lane who had sat through all this in silence, but ready and waiting.

Now her turn had come. 'Returning to the facts. Where did you spend those times when you were away from the site, supposedly playing the part of a dutiful son?'

Being questioned by a woman, it was strange to see the change in Lander's attitude. There was no hostility, but an increased wariness and he answered only after a significant pause. 'I was at Emile's cottage on the moor. We spent a lot of time there. Really, we shared the place and the cost.'

'So the mother who suffered from recurring attacks of migraine was just one more of your fantasies?'

'I'm afraid so.'

Wycliffe intervened. 'Were you at the cottage at all on Tuesday?'

A momentary hesitation, then, 'Yes I was.'

'At what time?'

'It must have been early evening. I didn't stay long.'

'Why did you go there?'

'I was bailing out, at least until things quietened down a bit. I wanted to pass the word, and recommend him to do likewise, but he wouldn't listen.'

'He was alone?'

'Oh yes. We didn't have visitors at the cottage.'

'What was he like? Was he worried? Depressed?'

'He was like a man waiting for the house to fall in on top of him but he wouldn't do anything about it.'

'He wasn't turning out his papers? Burning stuff – or preparing to?'

'I've told you: he wasn't doing anything.'

'When you heard that Emile was dead you assumed that he'd committed suicide and, in the circumstances, you were not all that surprised. Is that correct?'

'Yes, that is true.'

'Where did you spend Tuesday night?'

'I was in Torquay. As I said, I thought the whole situation was getting too difficult and I'd decided to move out.'

Wycliffe said, 'What you have told us needs to be checked. You will be detained for questioning for forty-eight hours. You will be taken to Penzance Police Station where you will be questioned by Detective Sergeants Lane and Boyd. DS Boyd is from our Drugs Squad.'

'That suits me. I'm in the clear.'

When Lander had been taken away Lucy said, 'Why did he come back?'

Wycliffe was thoughtful. 'Good question. He strikes me as an oddity – a really clever fool, and there are not many of them about. One could say that once he knew Collis was out of the way there was no longer anybody here in a position to make a formal accusation against him. He could turn up and tell his own tale, and that's what he's doing.'

Wycliffe contacted DS Boyd and put him in the picture. 'Lander is a consummate liar, Tim, but it's hard to know how far he's involved. DS Lane will bring you up to date. Any news from your end?'

Boyd said, 'We are working closely with Customs. We want news of what Lina did with her money. According to Customs, the likelihood is that she kept it over there. Of course their *weekeinde* is not much different from ours and we have to wait until they wake up bleary-eyed on Monday morning before we really get anywhere.'

Boyd went on, 'As far as Lander is concerned a lot depends on how much he gives this evening. Unless we have enough to charge him I suggest that we get authority to hold him for another forty-eight hours, by which time we should know where he fits in. I need photographs to circulate in the Torquay area. There's one on file which will do for the moment. It's largely a question of who sees them.'

'So where do we go from here?'

Wycliffe's conversation with Boyd was followed by a call from Forensic. In business on a Sunday!

'Regarding the clothing of Emile Collis, Dr Franks left word that you were interested in bloodstains on the front of the dead man's shirt. There were three spots of blood and they were approximately of the same age as the blood from the wound in his neck, but of a different group. Collis's blood was group A while the spots were from group AB.

'We can, of course, go further with this if you have any source for comparison.'

Wycliffe put down the telephone and passed on the news, 'So what we need, Lucy, is a source for comparison.'

'Would sir like to enlarge?'

'With pleasure. Franks suspected that the blood on Collis's shirt was not his. And he was right. Added to the scratches on his face the spots suggest that there was a struggle in which Collis's antagonist suffered what was probably a very minor injury.'

Lucy interrupted, 'You are saying then that Collis was murdered.'

'I've thought so all along and what Lander said didn't change my mind. For me there are just two questions, who? and when?'

Lucy said, 'According to Lander, backed up by Billy, he arrived and left in the early evening. And again, on Billy's word, we have Collis's car being driven off in the small hours. We know that it was dumped just outside New Mill at sometime during the night of Tuesday/Wednesday.'

Wycliffe agreed. 'And we considered the possibility that Collis had decided on a getaway, that he ran out of fuel, abandoned the car and returned to the cottage to make away with himself. To me, that is fantasy. The scratches on his face and the blood on his shirt-front alone are an answer to any such idea.'

'So?'

'I need to think.'

'Then I'll leave you to get on with it.'

It was evening, and Wycliffe was still in the police van. The sun had been shining all day with the sky a canopy of blue, but now clouds were creeping in from the west and the sun was already hidden.

The whole site was quiet. Presumably the residents were still around: Archer; Scawn the potter; Gew, the man of all work . . . Whatever happened in the future this, for the moment, was still their home. Presumably in the morning Alice Field would continue the furnishing of her little houses for the American market, and it was even possible that Paul would be at work in his carving shop.

All carried along for a little while by sheer momentum. But how long could it last?

Wycliffe was striving to relate the murder of Lina Archer in Collis's studio on Tuesday night to the discovery of Collis's body in his cottage on the following Saturday afternoon.

According to Franks Lina had died between ten and twelve on Tuesday night, while Collis had been dead for at least three, and possibly four days when he was found on the Saturday. In fact, all the evidence pointed to the likelihood that he too had died on the night of Tuesday/Wednesday.

The obvious interpretation, and the one relied upon by the killer, was that Collis had murdered Lina Archer then, after a desperate but futile attempt at escape, he had taken his own life.

But the latest evidence, that Collis had himself been a victim, was convincing, and the implication must be that the killer had gone straight from Collis's studio, where Lina Archer lay dead, to Collis's cottage.

And, in Wycliffe's view, the probability was that he had walked there.

He could not afford to risk driving a car off the site in the middle of the night nor, indeed, being seen on the road.

Lucy Lane returned to the van to find Wycliffe studying a 1/25000 map of the area. 'How far is it from here to Collis's cottage, Lucy?'

'Five and a half to six miles.' Lucy was tidying away the accumulated litter of the day.

'That's by road. If these paths are walkable it could be no more than two and a half.'

Lucy glanced at her watch. 'It's half-six already and I've got this interview with Lander in the Penzance nick.'

Wycliffe continued to study his map. 'You take the car. I'll get one of the patrols to pick me up when I'm ready. You'd better let them know at the hotel that we shall neither of us be in to dinner.'

'May one ask what you intend to do?'

'I'm planning a little walk.'

Lucy seemed about to say something but changed her mind and left.

The night guard was marking time, patrolling the site, waiting to settle in the van, but he would have to wait for another hour.

From the van Wycliffe could look across the site to the Archer house. The sky had clouded over entirely by now and already there was a light in a lower window.

It was eight o'clock when Wycliffe set out on his walk, his mobile in his pocket. He made a circuit, and arrived at the top of the slope above Collis's studio.

He was trying to imagine the state of mind of the man, the killer, when he left the studio that night with the body of Lina Archer lying lifeless on the floor. Only a little earlier the woman had been active, *involved*, and confident in her expectation of the days and years ahead.

He had he taken away her future. And the experience must have been many times more real, more immediate, than it had been with the girl, where his action had been remote from the event of her death.

Had he meant to kill for a second time? Almost certainly not. But anger and hatred and fear, and something more than all three, a kind of lust, had taken possession of him.

And what he must do next was determined by what he had already done.

He had no option.

The footpath Wycliffe had seen on the map snaked away through the heather and gorse, and in a very few minutes he had reached a road which, according to his map, must be Trewey Hill.

He had to pick up the footpath on the other side, and lost time because he was looking for a gap in the hedge instead of a primitive stile.

Once over the hedge the path was open to the moor so that if there had been anyone to see he would have been conspicuous, but the killer had had the protection of darkness.

Wycliffe trudged the moorland path, mainly uphill, for a mile or more, and came to the New Mill road.

Another crossing, another stile, and from the top of that stile Wycliffe could see Billy Ward's cottage against the skyline.

A dip, then a steep rise, a final stile, and he came out close to Billy's cottage, with the short lane to Collis's in front of him. The walk had taken him a little over forty minutes.

On that Tuesday the night had been clear and moonless, but Collis's car, parked in the lane, would have been dimly visible under the stars.

Now, although it was not yet dark, the light was poor. There was a light in Billy's cottage behind the drawn blind, and his collie gave a single sleepy bark, but that was all.

Wycliffe walked up the lane to Collis's door. He had a key and a torch, and he let himself in.

His torch-beam swept the dimly lit room. Fox had left it spick and span as though ready for Collis's return.

Wycliffe told himself that it was foolish to feel uneasy.

Of course Collis would have been there to greet his killer. Had he been troubled by the fact that his hideaway was known? Had he greeted his visitor with surprise? Or in fear? Was there immediate aggression? Or did they talk?

Wycliffe was sure that the attack, the blow to the base of Collis's skull, had taken place upstairs. Collis's body, unconscious or semi-conscious, had not been dragged or hauled, or even carried, up those narrow stairs without leaving traces for Fox to find.

The pretext by which the killer had got his victim upstairs would probably never be known.

But Wycliffe climbed the stairs. Unless he lit the paraffin lamps he had only his torch; and daylight was fading. Nothing seemed to have changed. Collis's framed pencil sketch of Francine still hung above the bed in the bedroom.

He felt sure that the blow when it came could not have been immediately and totally effective. It must have been at this point that the brief struggle occurred in which Collis's face had been scratched, and the blood spots from his attacker had stained his shirt-front.

But the killer had prevailed, and it was essential to create the impression of suicide. Collis was to hang himself, and the stairs provided the ideal setting.

Another period of action during which necessity was overtaken by obsessive involvement that was almost frenetic.

And then the burning, for which there could have been little if any purpose . . .

How long would it have taken the killer inside? Certainly not less than an hour and possibly two.

Then, if all this was more then a product of Wycliffe's imagination, the car had to be moved. The longer there was no obvious association between the cottage and the missing man, the more difficult it would be to determine the actual cause of death. Through it all the killer had kept in mind his own security.

And it had worked. Franks had been unable to pronounce between suicide and murder.

The keys of the car must have been taken from the body and the car driven away.

But the engine had died just to the south of New Mill. What would the killer have done if it hadn't?

In any case, presumably, he had had to walk home.

Wycliffe used his mobile to contact the Penzance nick and he gave them his position. Then, for twenty minutes, perched on a low wall, he was left to arrange his ideas into a credible pattern.

Of one thing he was now convinced: he knew who was responsible for the deaths of Francine Lemarque, Lina Archer and Emile Collis. There was no alternative. The blood tests would be significant evidence in support of a charge for the murder of Collis, but three spots of blood on a dead man's shirt would not go far in bringing charges for the other killings.

Well, tomorrow would be another day.

It was quite dark now. Billy had gone to bed, and light flared in the sky above St Ives on the one hand, and Penzance on the other.

No place for the old people.

Back at the hotel he joined Kersey and Lucy for a drink and a snack in the bar.

He seemed to have come from a different world and he tried almost frantically to adjust. 'Lander?'

Lucy said, 'We didn't get far. Tim Boyd persuaded him to give us some names – two of them people he claims to have been staying with in Torquay. One is a suspected dealer they've had an eye on for some time. Lander can be held for a further forty-eight hours and I've a strong feeling that is how he wants it. He's a slippery customer and he knows exactly how much to give.'

Wycliffe made no direct comment; he said simply, 'I want you to arrange a formal interview with Archer in the morning.'

Later, from his bedroom, he spoke to Helen.

Helen said, 'You sound odd. Is something wrong?'

'No, everything is fine.'

But he was a long time getting to sleep. His evening walk had, in a curious and most disturbing way, seemed to put him 'inside' the mind of the killer and he had glimpsed something of the man himself.

Or thought he had.

Chapter Thirteen

Monday

Another fine day. Wycliffe had slept little and he attended the morning's mini-briefing with almost nothing to say. The papers had reported the finding of Collis's body with photographs of the cottage, and several broad hints that this was the end of the trail as far as the Guild of Nine murders were concerned. Two of the papers mentioned a possible link with drug smuggling.

At the briefing most of the talking was left to Boyd. 'Dickie Mellor, from Customs, flew out last evening. The shop in the Oude Kerk has been under discreet observation since we passed word, and there will probably be a raid later today. Dutch financial guys are to start looking into the money set-up. Lander still maintains his innocence but we've authority to detain him for another forty-eight hours. He doesn't seem anxious to go anyway and I think the truth is that he feels safer with us.'

Wycliffe listened, and felt like a spectator.

In his office afterwards Lucy Lane reported that the Archer interview had been arranged for eleven o'clock.

'What was his attitude?'

'Reserved. I told him that he was entitled to be accompanied by a solicitor and he said there was no need.'

On the telephone Wycliffe made arrangements for an official from Forensic, in company with the police surgeon, to be available at the police station the following day to take a blood specimen from a suspect. The suspect's attendance would, in the first instance, be voluntary, but refusal might be met later with a Court Order.

Wycliffe wondered how much of his experiences of the previous night he would pass on to Lucy Lane. He had established nothing new; he had merely convinced himself, and he felt vaguely uncomfortable about the whole episode. He ended by giving her an edited version, and she seemed impressed. He summed up. 'Well, we shall see. In the Archer interview we will concentrate on the Collis case and see where it gets us.'

At eleven o'clock they were assembled in one of the interview rooms: Wycliffe, Lucy Lane and, of course, Archer.

Archer seemed to have lost weight, and his pink cheeks which had pouched slightly above his beard looked shrunken and pale. His hair had lost its sheen and much of its curl. He looked almost haggard.

Lucy Lane, in charge of recording, made the required introductions and handed over to Wycliffe.

Wycliffe said, 'Did you know that Collis was in possession of a cottage near Bodrifty where he spent much of the time that he was away from the Guild site?'

'No, I did not, not until the recent tragedy.'

'It seems that he was away quite often; sometimes overnight, and, occasionally, for whole weekends. Did it never occur to you to wonder where he spent his time? Surely it was the kind of thing you might have talked over with your wife?'

Archer hesitated. 'I suppose I might have been mildly curious but no more. I cannot recall discussing it with my wife. Members of our Guild work together, but they have their lives apart from the Guild.'

'You are acquainted with a man called Ward – Billy Ward, who occupies the cottage near Collis's. I understand that you visited him on one occasion to hear what he had to say about the Bronze and Iron Age people and their attitude to astrology.'

Archer looked surprised. 'That was some time ago, and he was unhelpful.'

'You did not at that time get any hint that Collis was in possession of the cottage close by?'

'I did not.'

'How did you get to Ward's place? Did you walk?'

Archer showed mild irritation. 'I went in my car. I don't understand— '

'I wondered if you were acquainted with the shortcut across the moor, virtually from your house to Billy Ward's – or to Collis's. I walked it last evening.'

Wycliffe allowed a brief interval and then changed his approach. 'I think I should tell you that yesterday I had a report from the pathologist on the autopsy he conducted on Collis's body. He could not decide whether Collis took his own life, or was murdered. As far as he is concerned the only indication of a possible struggle is that there were slight scratches on the dead man's face which *could* have been caused when and if he was responsible for the attack on your wife.'

Archer's arms rested on the table which separated him from Wycliffe, his hands clasped tightly together. 'So the cause of Collis's death is likely to remain in doubt?'

'In so far as the evidence from the pathologist is concerned – yes.'

There was a lengthy pause, then Archer, tentative, said, 'I would never have believed that Collis was capable of murder . . . '

Speaking slowly and quietly Wycliffe said, 'I know of no way of deciding who is and who is not capable of murder. I came into this case to investigate the death of Francine Lemarque. To the killer, who had never committed murder before, it must have seemed incredibly simple . . . In the final analysis it came down to a towel in the wrong place.'

Archer never took his eyes from Wycliffe's face but he murmured to himself, 'A towel in the wrong place.'

Wycliffe continued, 'Yes, put there with intent to murder, but there was a significant element of chance. What the killer did might, for several reasons, have failed to achieve its object. However, a little later the girl died, but by that time her killer may well have felt distanced from his crime.

'But the point is that a barrier had gone: murder had become possible. From that time on it would always be there, an ultimate solution.'

'So?' Archer spoke as though the word had been forced from his lips.

Wycliffe went on, 'It was my job to investigate her death. Now my investigation has broadened to cover the deaths of your wife and of Collis, as well as the systematic importation of illegal drugs.'

He shifted on his chair, which was uncomfortable. Archer did not move a muscle.

'Three people have died; two of whom were certainly murdered, while the third, Collis, *could* have taken his own life after bringing about the deaths of Francine and your wife. A bungled escape followed by suicide.'

When it seemed that the silence might continue indefinitely Archer said, in an oddly strained voice, 'You do not accept that explanation?'

Wycliffe was emphatic. 'No, I do not. Yesterday I heard from Forensic that bloodstains on the front of Collis's shirt were not of his blood, although they are of the same age as the other stains on his clothing.

'It is obviously possible that these stains came from an attacker, slightly injured in the struggle which rendered Collis unconscious.'

Archer said nothing and Wycliffe went on, 'It will be a simple matter to obtain specimens from those close to Collis for comparison.'

Archer seemed to consider what he would say, but said nothing.

'You have nothing to tell me, Mr Archer?'

'No.'

'Very well. Now that you are acquainted with all the facts you may need time to consider your position. This interview is over: it has been recorded and you will be asked to sign one of the tapes before leaving. A police car will take you home.'

When Archer had left Lucy said, 'What was the point? Within the next two or three days we could have positive evidence from Forensic of his presence at the cottage, and of his involvement with Collis.'

'A dubious foundation for a charge of triple murder, Lucy. Unless we can get him to talk we've still a long haul in front of us.'

A canteen lunch and by half-past one they were on their way to the Guild site; a drive that was becoming routine. As they passed the entrance sign he saw Alice Field, apparently at work as usual. Scawn would presumably be in his pottery, and Gew next door. The main door of the wood-carvers' shop was open, so presumably Paul was there. People wondering how to sort out their lives.

In the van, the duty PC said, 'Scawn has been here, sir. He's anxious to talk to you and he left his mobile number for me to call him when you are available.'

Wycliffe agreed and a few minutes later Scawn arrived.

'Sit down, Mr Scawn.'

With some difficulty Scawn folded himself into the van seat on one side of the table, facing Wycliffe and Lucy Lane on the other. Scawn was anxious and he began to speak at once.

'I'm afraid that I've held back certain information which, although it can hardly be relevant to anything that has happened, you may feel you should have had sooner.'

Wycliffe waited.

Scawn ran a hand through his dark hair. 'It concerns Mrs Archer – Lina.' There was a pause, then, 'We had a relationship.' His dark brown eyes searched the faces of his listeners for some reaction but found none.

Wycliffe said, 'You are speaking of a sexual relationship?'

'Yes.'

'Was Lander aware of this?'

Hesitation. 'It was never mentioned between us but in all the circumstances . . . Lina came to the flat, and although we were both very discreet it is probable that Lander was aware of what was happening.'

'And now that Lander is under some pressure you think that he may attempt to gain favour by passing on what he knows.'

Scawn said nothing.

'Does Archer know of your liaison with his wife?'

'Lina was quite sure that he did not. They did not share a bedroom. But in recent weeks I think he's been avoiding me, and when we have met he's been distant. Now, since Lina's death . . . '

Wycliffe took time to think. 'In your contacts with Lina Archer did she ever confide or discuss anything at all that might shed light on what happened to Francine?'

'No, she did not.'

'Did she ever say anything that even hinted at her involvement in the importation or handling of illegal drugs?'

'She certainly did not. All that came as a great shock to me.'

Wycliffe considered before speaking, then, 'I am going to ask you to put what you have told us into a formal statement which will only be used if at some time it appears to have direct relevance to our inquiry. DS Lane will be in touch.'

Scawn got up and stood for a moment, relieved but uncertain. 'I have no idea how free we are to leave the site. On Mondays I usually spend the evening with friends in Truro, returning at around midnight. Last Monday I put them off but I wondered about tonight.' A faint smile. 'I don't want to be posted as missing . . . '

Wycliffe said, 'There is no need to disappoint your friends, Mr Scawn.'

Another moment of hesitation, and Scawn left.

Lucy Lane said, 'Well, well! One way and another the flux seems to be getting pretty murky.'

Archer was alone in the house. Against opposition he had insisted on taking Evadne home earlier. Now it was dark, but he had not switched on any lights. He looked at the illuminated dial of his wristwatch. It was fifteen minutes to eleven. Plenty of time.

He let himself out, and closed the house door behind him, making sure that the lock had snapped shut. The night was clear and chilly, with a nor-easterly breeze, but he wore only a thin mackintosh. He had thought very carefully about this and decided that an overcoat might be a problem.

He left the site and walked down the track to the road. There he turned to the right, towards Zennor. A more or less straight stretch of road ran for perhaps two hundred yards to a sharp corner. On the seaward side there was a low drystone wall, on the other side the moor was bordered by a bank of ragged elder shrubs.

Archer knew precisely where he wanted to be. He trudged along the road to within a hundred yards or so of the corner, to a gap in the bushes where he could stand off the road.

He looked at his watch. It was almost five minutes past eleven. Plenty of time.

It was not really dark, because of the stars.

The stars. He could pick out the familiar constellations of the May sky . . . Better not to think along those lines.

He was surprised by his own calm. I am not even impatient . . . I am *composed*. He said the word aloud: 'Composed.'

The sea gleamed in the starlight and the coast line was a complex silhouette against the sea.

Archer wondered, *What shall I see afterwards?*

Will there be an afterwards?

Does it matter?

Wycliffe will have something to think about. He is a man of conscience, and he will be troubled. 'A towel in the wrong place' – those were his words. Now he will have, 'A man in the wrong place.'

He looked up and saw a glare of light above Eagle's Nest, then the headlights of a car cut great shafts into the night.

I must be sure.

The car swept down the hill and as it took the turn at the bottom Archer caught a glimpse of the Volvo's white chassis.

No doubt.

The corner, and the car accelerated. Fifty yards . . . Twenty . . . What would it be like?

An instant of excruciating pain . . .

And then?

It was three o'clock in the morning when Kersey, in a dressing-gown, woke Wycliffe from a disturbed sleep. 'I've just had a call from the duty officer at the nick, and I thought you should be told. There's been an accident on the coast road not far from the Guild site. It seems that a car, driven by Scawn, collided with a pedestrian who turns out to be our friend Archer. Archer is dead, and Scawn has been taken to hospital suffering from minor injuries and shock. It all sounds bloody odd to me.'

Wycliffe was already dressing. 'And to me. When did this happen?'

'They don't know exactly. It seems that Scawn, incoherent, arrived at one of the cottages scattered along the road and they phoned. Our lot and the ambulance arrived, but it took a while to dawn on some Einstein that the driver of the car was mixed up in our business and they went on from there.'

'What did you tell them?'

'To hold everything at the scene till we can take a look.'

'They will get the Vehicle people out there but you'd better get hold of Fox. I don't want any doubts about this.'

It was already broad daylight when they reached the coast road at the bottom of Trewey Hill where a PC was diverting what traffic there was.

A hundred yards along, the road was totally blocked by Scawn's Volvo slewed across it. The car's front bumper was half-buried in the rubble of a drystone wall: the radiator was damaged and dribbled water.

The police surgeon had visited the scene and, on the assumption that he was dealing with a road accident, he had allowed the body to be removed to the mortuary. The Vehicle examiners were there, and one was busy with a camera. Alan Turner, a uniformed inspector who had trained with Kersey, was in charge.

'I've never seen anything like it. The man was lying face-down, and the near-side front wheel actually went over his body. He was literally crushed to death. I can only think that he was drunk and fell asleep on the road.'

Turner gestured at the road ahead. 'This is one of the straighter stretches and the driver had probably just put his foot down.'

Wycliffe said nothing. Kersey called him to the near-side of the vehicle. There was no wall on this side, just a shrubby bank against the moor, and the ground between this and the car was littered and contaminated with the evidence of what had happened to Archer. The man's spectacle case was there, pathetically intact, a ballpoint pen . . . And the whole area was spattered with his blood and other, nameless, tissues.

It was then that Wycliffe noticed a gap in the thicket of elder bushes which bordered the road at this point. The gap was wide enough for a man to stand in, and there were signs that the grassy, peaty ground had been recently trampled.

He said to Kersey, 'I want this on record, Doug.' Then, to Turner, 'Where have they taken Scawn?'

'To Penzance hospital.'

Again to Kersey: 'I'm leaving you here, Doug. I'll keep in touch.'

Penzance was just coming to life for the new day; even the hospital had not yet got into its stride and a visitor was not welcomed.

'Yes, we do have a patient brought in after a car accident . . . You're from the police? . . . Very well, I'll check with Sister.'

Sister mobilised a young man in a white coat who looked fagged out. 'Dr Ruse. The police, about Mr Scawn.'

'We had him checked over. Minor superficial injuries but nothing dangerous. The surgeon is satisfied that he's not at risk . . . Yes, you can see him, but not too long. Remember he's in shock . . . '

Scawn's black hair and pale face on a white pillow. He opened his eyes, blinked, and sat up.

A word or two of sympathy.

'Yes, but I still can't believe what happened . . . He must have been standing by the roadside . . . I had a glimpse of his figure and of his face . . . He just threw himself in front of the car face-down . . . It was deliberate . . . This was no accident . . . I think I swerved in a useless attempt to avoid him but at the same moment there was a most awful crunch . . . I shall never forget it. Never!'

By nine o'clock Wycliffe was in the Incident Room, where he was joined by Lucy Lane. 'So you've been up most of the night?'

'Half of it.'

'I've heard the story. It's incredible!'

The morning mail was on Wycliffe's desk and he was going through it. He opened an envelope with a scrawled address. Inside there was a single sheet of paper which he spread on the desk for Lucy to read:

'Now you can have all the specimens you want but you can't prosecute a dead man. You will remember me as "The man who was always in the wrong place".'

Lucy was thoughtful. '*Is* that how you will remember him?'

Wycliffe took his time. 'No, it is not. In my opinion Archer was a man so obsessed by his own ideas that he would allow nothing to stand in their way. Not even another life.'

'You are thinking of the killing of Francine.'

'Yes. Because she had the means to threaten his precious Guild he decided to remove her, and he set about it with a chilling detachment that to me is the essence of wickedness.'

'But that was not how you put it to him.'

'No, because we needed to draw him out. We had, and we have, no material evidence to involve him in her death.'

'And the other two – his wife and Collis?'

'The difference was in motivation. When Archer discovered how he had been systematically deceived on all fronts he was tortured by a blend of hatred and fear and blinded to the risks he would run if he attempted revenge.'

They were interrupted by a great gust of wind which brought rain lashing against the window. 'There! They said we were in for a rough day. I only hope our people have finished on the road.'

The battering subsided and Wycliffe went on, 'I believe that Lina's murder was deliberate and that it was carried out with the intention of implicating Collis . . . It was a mad business, with risks at every stage.'

'But it almost worked.'

'It could still have worked. Apart from the blood on Collis's shirt which, incidentally, has yet to be identified as Archer's, we have little material evidence against him in any of the three deaths. It would have been a very long haul to build up a sustainable case, and with a good defence team he might have got away with all three killings . . . '

'So you gave him time and opportunity to talk himself into trouble. I wondered why you delayed his blood test. It could have been done yesterday.'

Wycliffe said nothing but continued going through his mail while Lucy turned over the pages of the report file.

It was Lucy who spoke first. 'Did it occur to you that he might take the problem out of our hands?'

It was some time before Wycliffe answered, and then he spoke slowly. 'I did not for one moment imagine that he would involve someone else.' There was a pause before he added, 'And that's all I'm going to say, Lucy.'

A Sunday afternoon six months later

With no murder trial pending, and the investigation into heroin smuggling having lost its first dramatic impact, the Guild and its members had been forgotten by the press.

Wycliffe was turning the pages of the local weekly while Helen read a novel. Outside it was raining. Wycliffe spotted a minor headline: 'Guild of Nine Revival?'

'Listen to this.' He read the report aloud:

Our correspondent has learned that the lease of the property on the moor near St Ives, occupied by the Guild of Nine, has been acquired by Paul Bateman, the distinguished wood carver, with the intention of creating a new craft centre.

Paul Bateman, a member of the Guild, will be joined by three of his former colleagues and by Hugh Marsden, a near neighbour, and long-established figure in the field of landscape painting.

Helen said, 'Well?'

'What can one say except to wish 'em luck? Marsden has

probably done Paul a lot of good . . . But there will never be another Francine.'

Helen returned to her book. 'Odd, your attitude to that girl, considering that in her short life she caused so many people so much grief.'